LAW OF THE FRONTIER

Deputy US Marshal Morgan Cassidy took leave to answer his mother's call for help after his father is murdered. When Morgan arrived at the ranch he found his mother had also died in mysterious circumstances, and the family's Box C Ranch was now in the hands of Kennedy, owner of the big Crazy R Ranch, adjacent to the Box C. Morgan strongly suspected Kennedy and his hired gunmen were responsible for the deaths, but with the rancher and his men gunning for him, Morgan's problem was how to stay alive long enough to deliver the guilty men to the law...

LAW OF THE FRONTIER

LAW OF THE FRONTIER

by

Alan Irwin

Dales Large Print Books
Long Preston, North Yorkshire,
BD23 4ND, England.

British Library Cataloguing in Publication Data.

Irwin, Alan
    Law of the Frontier.

    A catalogue record of this book is
    available from the British Library

    ISBN   1-84262-136-X pbk

First published in Great Britain 2001 by Robert Hale Ltd.

Published in Large Print 2002 by arrangement with
Robert Hale Limited

Dales Large Print is an imprint of Library Magna Books Ltd.

Printed and bound in Great Britain by
T.J. (International) Ltd., Cornwall, PL28 8RW

To Betty Burke

One

Riding in a westerly direction through Kansas, close to the border with Indian Territory, and not far west of Caldwell, Morgan Cassidy paused as he reached a stretch of high ground from which he could look down into the narrow valley below.

He could see, immediately below him, a single homestead stretching back from the east bank of the river, with neatly fenced fields and a cluster of outbuildings close to the two-storey house.

He dismounted and lifted his mount's foreleg to look at a front shoe which had worked loose. Despite his urgent need for haste, he knew that it needed attention before he rode any further. There was a good chance that the homesteader down below would have the necessary equipment to make at least a temporary repair.

He led his big bay gelding down the slope and along the rough track between two of the fields which led to the house. As he approached it he could see three saddled horses tied to a hitching rail near to the building. Reaching the rail, he dismounted, tied his horse to it, and looked around. There was no one in sight.

He walked up to the door and knocked on it. He caught a glimpse of somebody looking through a window close to one side of the door, and shortly afterwards the door was pulled open and a man stood in the doorway.

He was holding a revolver in his right hand, pointed at Morgan's chest. He was a big man, roughly dressed and bearded. There was a mean look in his eye which kept Morgan's hand well away from the handle of his Colt .45 Peacemaker.

The man, keeping Morgan covered, moved back and to one side.

'Step inside,' he said.

It was more an order than an invitation, and as Morgan obeyed him and walked past the man into the house, he felt his Peacemaker being lifted from its holster. Two paces inside the room he stopped and heard the door close behind him.

There were six people in the room, excluding himself and the man behind him. Two of the six, both men, were seated at a table, obviously in process of taking a meal. They had turned in their seats and were observing him closely.

One thing was certain, thought Morgan. These two and the man at his back were not homesteaders. He felt sure that such a tough- and dangerous-looking trio must be criminals.

They were, in fact, the three members of the Dolan Gang, wanted for multiple robberies and killings in Kansas and Nebraska. The leader, Pat Dolan, sat at the table. A thickset man in his forties, of average height, bearded and beetle-browed, he had a reputation as a merciless killer when crossed or threatened.

His companion at the table was Frank Riley, a thin, weasel-faced man, older than Dolan. The man holding a gun on Morgan's back was Pete Baldwin, a man in his late thirties, with long hair reaching down to his shoulders.

Morgan looked at the remaining four people in the room, all seated on the floor with their backs to the wall on the far side of the room. A middle-aged man and woman, Ben and Mary Gardner, with their son Joey, aged ten and their daughter Marion, in her early twenties, they all stared across at Morgan. It was clear to him that this must be the homesteader and his family.

Ben Gardner wondered who the stranger was and why he had called in at the homestead. Studying Morgan closely, he saw a man in his late twenties, clean-shaven, well-built, and a little above average height. He didn't look unduly worried about the gun at his back and there was an air of confidence about him.

Dolan spoke to Gardner. 'You know this man?' he asked.

Gardner shook his head.

Dolan addressed Morgan. 'What's your business here, stranger?' he asked.

'My horse has a loose front shoe,' replied Morgan. 'I figured maybe I could get some help here fixing it well enough to get me to the next blacksmith along the trail.'

'You're out of luck, dropping in here,' said Dolan. 'See if he's got any more weapons hidden away, Frank, and check his pockets for cash.'

Riley searched Morgan thoroughly. He found no weapons, but handed Dolan a roll of banknotes from the prisoner's vest pocket. The gang leader grinned as he counted the bills.

'Well, well,' he said, 'it sure was our lucky day when you rode in here. This is a lot better than the measly thirty five dollars we got from these settlers. There must be close on five hundred dollars here. Just sit down against the wall there.'

Morgan sat down, facing Gardner and his family.

'Anybody getting up without my say-so is liable to get plugged,' said Dolan, and the three outlaws, keeping a close watch on the prisoners, continued with the interrupted meal.

Looking across at the homesteaders Morgan was struck by the beauty of the young woman. She was slender, with fine features and hazel eyes, framed by auburn shoulder-length hair. She favoured her mother, now grey-haired, sitting on the floor beside her.

Morgan noticed that Dolan's eyes kept straying to Marion and he could see that the homesteader and his wife and daughter were, with growing concern, also aware of the outlaw's attention.

Morgan was sitting against the wall, with his right shoulder against the side of an open cupboard fitted with shelves up to the ceiling. He noticed that Gardner, without moving his head, was alternately staring at him intently, then shifting his eyes downwards and to Morgan's right.

Surreptitiously, Morgan turned his head slightly down and to the right, and close to him, at the back of the bottom shelf, he could see the handle of a revolver. It was out of sight of the outlaws. Looking back at Gardner he gave a slight nod, then looked over towards the outlaws, who were getting up from the table.

While Dolan watched the prisoners, his eyes lingering on Marion in particular, Riley and Baldwin filled two sacks with provisions taken from a small storeroom built in the corner of the room. When this was done Riley turned to the gang leader.

'Are we leaving now?' he asked.

'Soon,' replied Dolan, 'and we'll take those two horses in the corral with us. Maybe they'll come in handy if that posse gets anywhere near. But before we leave,' he went on, his eyes on Marion, 'there's something I've a mind to do.'

He walked over to a door in the wall of the

room and opened it wide. Morgan could see that it was a bedroom. Dolan turned and looked at Marion again. As she cringed at the lustful leer on his face, her mother put an arm around her.

'The girl there,' said Dolan to his men. 'Before we go, I've a mind to get better acquainted with her. She sure is a welcome sight for anybody who's been on the run as long as we have. Keep an eye on the others, both of you.'

As Dolan advanced towards Marion, stretching out a hand with the intention of grabbing her and pulling her to her feet, she cried out and shrank back against the wall. Her father started to rise to his feet, but sank down again as a bullet from Riley's six-gun slammed into the wall a couple of inches to one side of his head.

Seeing that all three outlaws were looking towards Gardner and his daughter, Morgan reached down with his right hand to pick the revolver off the shelf. As he grasped the handle and raised the six-gun, Dolan advanced on the girl again, while Riley stood watching, holding his revolver in his hand.

Still seated, Morgan shot Dolan in the back before the outlaw reached the girl. He immediately recocked his gun and shot Riley in the chest as the startled outlaw, raising his gun, swung round to face him.

As Morgan fired his first shot, Baldwin drew his gun and turned. But he was slightly behind Riley, who staggered backwards into him under the impact of Morgan's bullet. By the time Baldwin had recovered, Morgan was ready to fire his third shot and both men fired simultaneously as Riley slumped to the floor between them.

Baldwin, hit in the chest, dropped his gun, twisted round, fell against the wall close to Gardner, then slid down to the floor. The homesteader bent forward and picked up the gun.

The bullet from Baldwin's six-gun had gouged a furrow along the side of Morgan's head before embedding itself in the wall. Morgan slumped sideways to the floor and lay motionless.

Gardner rose to his feet and collected the guns belonging to Riley and Dolan. He dropped them on the floor on the far side of the room. Then he bent over the three outlaws in turn as his wife and children, badly shaken by the sudden turn of events, rose to their feet.

'I reckon these two are dead,' he said, pointing to Riley and Dolan. 'The other one's still breathing but he's been hit bad. I'm pretty sure there's a bullet inside him. He ain't able to do us no harm.'

The two women knelt down by the side of Morgan. His eyes were closed and he was breathing heavily. He appeared to be unconscious. Mary Gardner closely examined the wound along the side of his head. It was bleeding, but not profusely. She sent Marion for a cloth and some warm water, and bathed the wound. Then she attempted to staunch the flow of blood.

'We owe this man plenty,' said Gardner. 'It took a lot of grit to take on these three. I sure hope he ain't hurt bad.'

He turned to Marion. 'Ride into Barstow, Marion,' he said. 'I'm pretty sure Sheriff Benson's going to be in town today. Tell him what's happened here. Ask him and Doc Bradley to come out to the homestead right away.'

When Marion had left, her mother had a look at Baldwin. He was still alive. She could see where the bullet had entered his chest and decided there was nothing she could do for him before the doctor arrived.

An hour and a half passed before Marion returned with the doctor and the sheriff. Morgan was still unconscious. Looking down at the outlaws, Benson recognized them immediately.

'This is the Dolan Gang,' he said. 'The law's been after them for quite a while. Only a few days ago they robbed a bank in Ellsworth. Killed a cashier and rode off with a posse after them, but they got clear away.'

The doctor took a quick look at Morgan, then he examined Baldwin. 'This bullet has to come out,' he said, 'if this man's to have the slightest chance of living.'

With Mary Gardner's help he cleaned up the wound and sterilized his instruments. Then he started probing the wound and finally located the bullet, but the outlaw died as he was trying to remove it.

The doctor turned his attention to Morgan. 'D'you know who this man is?' he asked Gardner.

The homesteader shook his head. 'He's a stranger to us,' he said. 'He was just passing by. Lucky for us he called in. And luckier still that he's so handy with a six-gun. He sure surprised those three outlaws.'

Doctor Bradley knelt down and bent over Morgan. 'How long has he been unconscious?' he asked Mary Gardner.

'Must be nearly two and a half hours,' she replied.

Bradley examined Morgan closely, checking his reflexes in the process. Then he looked at the others.

'Sometimes,' he said, 'a head injury can

cause damage to the brain and sometimes that damage can result in a coma. I reckon that's what's wrong with this man.'

'When's he likely to come out of it?' asked Gardner.

'It ain't possible for me to say,' replied the doctor, as he put a bandage around Morgan's head. 'It depends on the amount of the damage. Can he stay here?'

'Of course he can,' said Mary Gardner. 'He wouldn't be like this if he hadn't risked his life to save us. Maybe the sheriff would help you to carry him through to that bed in the room over there, Ben. And let us know, Doctor, how we should look after him.'

When Morgan had been moved, Gardner and the sheriff dragged the three dead outlaws into the barn to await a buckboard which would take them into town.

'I'm hoping,' the doctor said to the Gardners before departing with the sheriff, 'that the man who helped you out will come around in a day or two. When he does, let me know right away.'

Two

It was in the middle of the morning, two days after he had been shot, when Morgan's eyes opened and he moved his head. Marion, who had just walked into the room to look at him, ran off to bring her mother. The two women stood looking down at him. Gardner and Joey were out in one of the fields.

Morgan looked up at them without any sign of recognition, then raised himself to a sitting position and looked around.

'Where am I?' he asked.

'Why, you're on our homestead,' said Mary Gardner. 'Don't you remember? When you called in a couple of days ago there were three outlaws in here and one of them shot at you. The bullet grazed the side of your head.'

Morgan raised his hand and felt the bandage around his head. He frowned.

'I don't remember,' he said, slowly.

'What's your name?' she asked.

'I don't remember that either,' he said. 'I don't remember anything that happened before I woke up just now.'

'Marion,' said her mother. 'Tell your father what's happened, then ride into town and tell Doc Bradley. Ask him to come out here. Meanwhile I'll get some food ready for the patient. It's a while since he had a good meal. And I'll tell him exactly how he comes to have this head wound.'

By the time Marion returned with the doctor, Morgan had left the bed and had taken a meal. He was feeling better, but he told Bradley that he still had no recollection of events prior to his coming out of the coma. Nor could he remember his name or anything about his family.

The doctor told Morgan that he had made enquiries in Barstow, but nobody there had any recollection of seeing him in town. Then he took a look at the wound on Morgan's head.

'That's healing up fine,' he said. 'As for the loss of memory, there's a good chance it'll all come back soon. Just when, I can't say. Just take it easy while that wound's healing. I'll come out to see you later in the week.'

When the doctor had left, Morgan looked through the pockets in his clothing. There was nothing there which gave the remotest clue as to his identity. He asked Gardner which horse he had arrived on, then walked over to the bay, which was grazing in the pasture. It wasn't branded and a search of the saddle-bags proved fruitless.

Slowly, Morgan walked back to the house. Somewhere, in the dim recesses of his mind, was a feeling that there was something important he must attend to. But what that something was he could not recall, however hard he tried. He felt completely helpless, and not a little scared, as he contemplated the immediate future.

The Gardners were all in the house when

he returned. He spoke to Gardner and his wife.

'It looks like I'd better hang around for a while,' he said, 'until my memory comes back. I don't even know which direction I was riding in when I called in here. But I don't want to put on you no more. I'll get a room in the hotel in Barstow.'

'You'll do no such thing!' said Mary Gardner. 'Not after what you done for us. We want you to stay here till your mind clears up.' Her husband nodded emphatically in agreement.

'I'm mighty obliged to you,' said Morgan, 'for that invitation. And I'm going to accept it. But only if you let me help out on the homestead while I'm here.'

'Just around now,' said Gardner, 'is a busy time for me. My family helps me as much as they can, but I can do with any extra help I can get.'

At Morgan's request the homesteader gave details of the work he could help with, and accordingly, for the next four weeks,

Morgan helped out on various jobs around the homestead. All the time, he had the vague feeling that he should be somewhere else, but there was no sign of his memory returning.

As well as their parents, both Marion and Joey welcomed Morgan's presence on the homestead and twice he had accompanied the settler's daughter into Barstow to pick up supplies. She was a lively, intelligent girl and he found himself enjoying her company.

At the beginning of the fifth week of his stay he once again drove the buckboard into town, accompanied by Marion and Joey.

'I can't imagine how you feel,' said Marion, 'not knowing who you are.'

'It's a mighty strange feeling,' said Morgan. 'Looking at my hands it's pretty clear I ain't been using them for farming or looking after cattle. And it seems I'm pretty handy with a gun.

'I've got to admit that I don't feel dressed out proper without one, and when I pull my Peacemaker from the holster it comes out smooth and quick and it fits real snug into my hand. I'm hoping that I don't turn out to be a gunfighter and an outlaw.'

'I can't imagine that,' said Marion, 'not after the way you helped us out. You've still got no idea where you came from?'

'Not a glimmer,' replied Morgan, 'and I'm wondering if I've got kinfolk somewhere who're wondering where I am. Just now and again I get a hazy memory of being a young child and then a boy somewhere, with a father and mother around, but I've no idea where that "somewhere" is. And I've got no idea why I turned up here.

'If my memory don't come back soon I figure to start riding around to try to find somebody who knows me. I'll start with Caldwell and the other cowtowns. It's a good thing I was carrying all that cash with me.'

When they reached Barstow Marion and Joey went into the general store, while Morgan stayed on the seat of the buckboard. After a while Ridley, the storekeeper, carried several sacks and boxes out on to the boardwalk and Morgan climbed down to help load the items on to the buckboard. As he stepped up on to the boardwalk Marion and Joey came out of the store.

Morgan paused and looked along the street as he heard the muffled sound of a gunshot. Moments later, the door of the small bank a little way along the street burst open and a masked man dashed out holding a sack in his left hand and a Colt .45 in the other. The top of the sack was held closed by a length of cord. The man was an outlaw called Matlock, a ruthless killer who specialized in single-handed bank and stagecoach robberies.

The outlaw ran to his horse which was standing at a hitching rail close by, then paused and fired towards the doorway of the bank, in which an elderly man had appeared. As the bullet struck the timber door frame and lodged there the man in the doorway hastily retreated inside the bank.

Matlock quickly hung the sack on the

pommel of his saddle. Then he mounted his horse and urged it along the street in the direction which would take him past the store and out of town to the north. He was watching closely for any sign of armed intervention to prevent his departure.

Morgan drew his Peacemaker and calmly stepped down off the boardwalk to face the mounted man who was approaching him at speed. He raised the Peacemaker.

Matlock spotted him and fired three shots at him from the back of the moving horse. All three bullets missed their target. Morgan stood motionless, ignoring the fire, until he had a clear view of the outlaw's upper body. Then, following the moving target with the muzzle of his pistol, he planted a single bullet in Matlock's right shoulder.

The outlaw dropped his revolver, jerked backwards, and lost his seat in the saddle. He fell sideways off his horse to the ground. For a few yards one of his feet was held in the stirrup. Then it came free.

Matlock lay on the ground, cursing, and

holding his right shoulder. The mask had become dislodged during his fall. He looked up as Morgan approached and stood over him. Along the street his horse was stopped by a couple of townsmen.

The storekeeper came and stood alongside Morgan. A small crowd collected and stared down at the wounded outlaw. Marion and Joey watched from the buckboard.

'I reckon,' said Ridley, 'that this man's an outlaw called Matlock. I've seen his face on a Wanted poster.'

'Is the sheriff around?' asked Morgan.

'Not today,' replied Ridley. 'He ain't stationed here. But likely he'll be calling in tomorrow.'

The elderly man from the bank hurried up to them. He was Harvey, the bank manager. The men who had stopped the outlaw's horse came up and handed him the sack which Matlock had carried out of the bank. Harvey carefully checked the contents then turned to Morgan.

'Every man and woman in and around this

town,' he said, 'should be grateful to you. They've worked long and hard for the money in that sack. It was quite a risk you took, stopping him like that.'

'I figured,' said Morgan, 'that accurate shooting from the back of a running horse just ain't possible. Was anybody hurt in the bank?'

'The cashier,' replied Harvey. 'Doc Bradley's looking at him now. But I reckon he's dead.'

The doctor came up as Harvey finished speaking. 'The cashier's dead,' he said. He bent down over the outlaw and examined the wound in his shoulder.

'There's a bullet in there needs to be taken out,' he said. 'Better bring him to my place.'

Ridley turned to Morgan.

'I work as a temporary deputy under Sheriff Benson now and again,' he said. 'I'll take charge of Matlock until the sheriff gets here. Likely he'll come out to the homestead for a few words with you about the

31

shooting when he gets here.'

On the way back to the homestead Marion spoke about the recent events in town.

'That robber,' she said. 'While you stood waiting for him to come close, we were sure he was going to shoot you down.'

'I just had the feeling,' said Morgan, 'that that was the right thing to do if I wanted to stop him from getting away. I felt like I'd been under fire before. And just as the shooting finished I felt it was on the point of bringing my memory back. Maybe another little jolt of some sort will do the trick.'

'I've been thinking,' said Marion, 'about what you might have been doing before you called at the homestead. Maybe you were a lawman.'

'Maybe you're right,' said Morgan. 'I sure hope I find out before long.'

'When your memory does come back,' asked Marion, 'and if it turns out you ain't a married man, are we likely ever to see you again?'

'It depends on you, Marion,' he replied.

'I'd sure like to call back here to see you.'

She smiled. 'You'll always be welcome,' she said.

The following morning Morgan was doing some work in the barn. A strong wind outside was intermittently howling around the structure. Hearing Gardner calling him from outside, Morgan pushed the heavy door wide open, took a step outside, and looked in the homesteader's direction.

Gardner shouted a warning as, after a brief lull in the wind, the door was caught squarely by a powerful gust and swung towards Morgan. As it slammed into the back of his right shoulder he was propelled violently forward and sideways. Losing his balance, he twisted and fell on his back on the ground, hitting the back of his head in the process.

He lay still for a few moments as Gardner ran towards him. Then he sat up, holding his head in his hands.

'You all right?' asked the homesteader, helping Morgan to his feet.

'It's happened,' said Morgan, slowly. 'My memory. It's coming back.'

'Come inside and sit down,' said Gardner, 'and tell us all about it.'

Five minutes later, sitting in the living-room with the Gardner family, Morgan knew that his memory had fully returned.

'My name's Morgan Cassidy,' he told them. 'For three years now I've been a deputy US marshal working in Indian Territory, with headquarters in Fort Smith, Arkansas. I was in the Territory, not far south of here, when a message was sent on to me from Fort Smith.

'It was from my mother, Sarah Cassidy. She sent it from the Box C Ranch in Colorado which my father had been running for the past five years. It was a short message. It read: "Your father murdered. Need you back. Mother."

'I was given leave of absence right away and I was on my way to the ranch when I called here. I've got to leave for Colorado right away. My mother's bound to be worried sick, me not having turned up there yet.'

Marion and her mother hurried to prepare a meal for Morgan and to put some provisions together for him to take along with him.

'I'll explain to Sheriff Benson where you've gone if he turns up here looking for you,' said Gardner.

Three

Three days later Morgan rode west along the south bank of the Arkansas River, heading for the Box C range, just a few miles ahead. As he rode along he noticed that the range bordering the Box C spread was well stocked with cattle. He rode up to a cow and saw that it was wearing a Crazy R brand. Obviously another rancher was now operating in the area.

He rode on until he crossed into Box C range. Four miles further on he came to the Box C ranch house. There was, he thought, a rather neglected look about the place.

Two men standing outside the house watched him closely as he rode up. Both men were strangers to him. He wondered who they were.

'Howdy,' he said. 'Is Mrs Cassidy inside?'

One of the men replied. He was a big man, bearded and surly-looking. His name was Barlow.

'There ain't no Mrs Cassidy here,' he said. 'What's your business?'

'I'm here to see Mrs Cassidy,' said Morgan. 'I'm her son. Where is she?'

Barlow and his companion looked at one another. Then Barlow spoke. 'She's dead,' he said. 'She was drowned in the river about three weeks ago.'

Badly shocked, Morgan was silent for a few moments. Then he spoke again. 'Did you work for her?' he asked.

'We work for Kennedy,' replied Barlow. 'He's the owner of the Crazy R.'

'What're you doing here on the Box C?' asked Morgan.

'This spread belongs to Kennedy now,' replied Barlow. 'Your mother sold it to him over three weeks ago, together with the cows. Have you heard about your father?'

'I have,' said Morgan, greatly puzzled by his mother's sale of the ranch and severely shaken by the news of her death. 'I'm going into Dennison now. I'll stay there a while and likely I'll be calling on Kennedy soon.'

Dennison lay by the river, five miles further upstream from the Box C ranch house. When Morgan reached the edge of town he headed for the small general store run by his aunt, Betty Burke. Betty, a spirited lady, was his mother's sister, and the two women had always been very close. Betty had decided to move West with her sister and brother-in-law and when she found there was no proper store in town she decided to open one.

A slim, normally vivacious woman in her fifties, Betty looked up from behind the counter as Morgan walked into the store. Her jaw dropped and she burst into tears as she saw him. There had always been a strong bond of affection between them.

She ran from behind the counter into his arms. He held her until she had pulled herself together, then she put a CLOSED notice on the door and they went through into the living-room and sat down.

'Morgan!' she said. 'Your mother and me just couldn't figure out why you didn't turn up at the ranch. We heard you were on your way, but you never arrived.'

Morgan explained to his aunt the reason for his late response to his mother's call for help. He told her that he had found two Crazy R ranch hands at the Box C ranch house who told him that his mother had sold the ranch to Kennedy. Then he asked her to tell him exactly what had happened, starting with his father's death.

'I'll go back a bit earlier than that,' she said. 'I think trouble started brewing about a year ago when Kennedy bought a big stretch of land along the river on both sides of the Box C. He brought in a herd and started ranching in a really big way.'

She went on to tell Morgan that soon after his arrival Kennedy had offered to buy the Box C, but Morgan's father had turned him down flat then, and had also rejected later offers.

Walt Cassidy's death had taken place close to the river, between the Box C and Dennison, when the rancher was riding alone to the ranch after a visit to town. He'd been killed by a bullet from a rifleman waiting in ambush in a small grove of trees close to the trail. His body had been found some time later by Jardine, one of his hands.

With the nearest lawman a hundred miles away, Jardine and Clark, the other Box C hand, had searched the grove and found the place where the killer had hidden. An empty rifle-cartridge case was lying nearby and they had seen the blurred tracks of a man and a horse in the soft ground inside the grove. There was nothing distinctive about the tracks and they were unable to follow them for any distance outside the grove.

They found nothing that would help them to identify the killer and he got away scot-free. It turned out later that two hundred dollars in banknotes that Walt had picked up at the bank earlier in the day were not on the body when it was found.

According to Kennedy, said Betty, an armed stranger had been seen riding across his range not long before the shooting and he figured that this man must have been the one who shot and robbed Morgan's father.

'Did mother have any ideas about who the killer might be?' asked Morgan.

'No,' replied Betty. 'At the time, she was just as puzzled as everybody else.'

She went on to tell how, three days after the funeral, Kennedy had ridden up to the Box C ranch house and had made Sarah an offer for the ranch which she had declined, telling him that she intended to carry on running the place herself. 'She told him that she'd already sent a message to you asking you to come home.'

Kennedy, a big, overbearing man, bearded, with beetling eyebrows and an abrupt manner, hadn't appeared to take Sarah's refusal kindly. He told her that he would be calling again soon to see if she had changed her mind.

'When your mother and I talked about it

on the day after Kennedy had called at the Box C,' said Betty, 'she told me that she thought Kennedy was trying to scare her, and after he'd left she began to wonder if he'd had anything to do with the killing. But she was expecting you to turn up in two or three days' time and she decided to wait till you got here before mentioning the idea to anybody but me.

'And that was the last time I saw her alive. As for her selling the ranch to Kennedy, I just don't believe it. I'm certain she'd have discussed it with me first if that's what she was thinking of doing.'

'And how did mother come to die?' asked Morgan.

Betty told him that three days after Kennedy's visit, his mother's body had been found on Crazy R range by Kennedy and his foreman Hartley. It was floating in some shallows about three miles downstream from the Box C ranch house. There was a nasty bruise on her head. She'd been all right when her two hands had left her early in the morning.

'The river was running pretty deep and fast at the time,' said Betty, 'and the general feeling was that Sarah had accidentally fallen down that steep stretch of bank near the ranch house and her head had been bruised either on the way down or when she was floating down the river.

'But thinking about what your mother told me about Kennedy, I began to wonder if he could have had a hand in both the deaths; what do you think, Morgan?'

'I haven't met Kennedy yet,' said Morgan, 'so it's hard for me to judge. But I think there's a chance you might be right. My job now is to find out the truth, one way or the other.'

'While you're doing that,' said Betty, 'I'd like you to stay here with me.' She told him that his mother was lying beside his father in the small cemetery just outside town.

Morgan rode out to the cemetery and stood beside the graves for a while. Then he rode back to the livery stable in the middle of town. The owner, Hal Jenkins, was standing outside. He started as he recognized Morgan, who had spent two years on the Box C before becoming a lawman in Indian Territory.

Morgan knew that Jenkins and his father had been good friends, and after greeting the liveryman he explained his late arrival on the scene and asked Jenkins if he could put his horse up and spare the time for a few words.

'Sure,' said the liveryman. 'Come inside.'

When the horse had been attended to, they stood talking just inside the stable door.

'This business of my father and mother both being found dead, Hal,' said Morgan. 'You got any ideas how it might have happened?'

'First,' said Jenkins, 'I want to say how sorry I am they're gone. They were both good friends of mine. Your father helped me out with a loan when I was having a hard time setting this business up. If it hadn't been for him it would have failed. I've sure been missing them lately.

'As for your father's death, it's a mystery who gunned him down. And nobody can tell for certain how your mother came to be in the river.'

'You know that Kennedy claims my mother sold him the Box C?' asked Morgan.

'Yes,' Jenkins replied. 'His men spread the news around the day after she was found dead. Everybody was real surprised to hear about it. We all figured she'd have waited till you turned up before deciding on anything like that.'

'According to Aunt Betty,' said Morgan, 'Mother had a notion that maybe Kennedy was so set on getting his hands on the Box C that he was responsible for my father's death.'

Startled, Jenkins stared at Morgan.

'And if,' continued Morgan, 'Kennedy was enough of a villain to have my father murdered, then ain't it likely he'd want to get rid of my mother as well, when he found

45

she wasn't willing to sell?'

'But she *did* sell,' said Jenkins.

'Did she?' asked Morgan. 'Do we have real proof of that? I reckon I'll go along to the bank and see if the manager knows anything about the sale.'

'Kennedy ain't popular around here,' said Jenkins. 'He ain't a man you can warm to. Seems to think he's a cut above the rest of us. But I'm finding it hard to believe that he's a double murderer.'

'Maybe I'm wrong,' said Morgan, 'but I'm going along to the bank now. Is Dawson still the manager?'

'Yes, he is,' replied Jenkins.

'What I've just said, keep it to yourself,' asked Morgan.

As he approached the bank, a little way along the street from the livery stable, a man came out of the door, looked at Morgan, then quickly turned and walked away from him along the boardwalk. Morgan recognized him as Barlow, the Crazy R hand he had met at the Box C ranch house

46

earlier in the day.

Morgan went into the bank and asked the cashier if he could see the manager. The cashier took him to a small office at the rear of the building. Dawson was seated at a desk inside. He was a slim, well-dressed, middle-aged man, with greying hair, a neat moustache and an impressive air of integrity. He looked up as Morgan was ushered in, then rose to his feet. His face was solemn as he shook Morgan's hand.

'Mr Cassidy,' he said. 'Please accept my deepest sympathy in your double loss. The whole town has been shocked by the terrible events of the past weeks.'

'Thanks,' said Morgan. 'I've been some shocked myself. And I sure was surprised when I heard from two Crazy R hands that my mother had sold the Box C to Kennedy. I've called in to see if you know anything about the deal.'

'Of course,' said Dawson. 'Mr Kennedy asked me to help him with the transaction, so I drew up the papers and he and I rode out to the ranch two days after Kennedy made his first offer to your mother. Kennedy made her a better offer than before and she decided to accept it. She signed the papers and Kennedy handed over the money in banknotes.

'The arrangement was that she would hand over the ranch four weeks later. I strongly advised her to place the money in the bank, but she insisted on keeping it with her. As for the price, it seemed to me that Kennedy's offer was reasonable.'

Morgan studied Dawson's face. Although the banker's account of events was given in an entirely convincing manner, and although, as far as Morgan knew, his reputation was impeccable, he found it hard to believe what Dawson had just told him.

'I wonder where the money is now,' said Morgan, 'and I can't figure out why my mother didn't wait till I turned up before selling the ranch.'

'Your mother was a strong-minded woman, Mr Cassidy,' said Dawson. 'I suggested that she might wait for you. But it was no good. She'd already made up her mind, she said. As for the money, I've no idea what she did with it after we left.

'Maybe you'd better ask Kennedy if it was found in the ranch house by him or his men. If it was, I'm sure he'll be holding it for you.'

'Yes, I'll do that,' said Morgan. 'What time of day was it when you and Dawson visited my mother on the Box C?'

'It was early afternoon,' replied Dawson. 'We left there around three o'clock.'

Morgan thanked the banker, left the bank, and walked back along the street, past the livery stable, to Doc Garrett's house. Garrett, a kindly, conscientious, middle-aged man, had been a friend of the family ever since they settled in the area.

He answered Morgan's knock on the door and invited him inside.

'Heard you were in town,' he said. 'I'm real sorry about what happened to your parents. It just don't bear thinking about.'

'I aim to get to the bottom of it all,' said Morgan. 'Did you see the bodies before they were buried?'

'I did,' replied Garrett. 'The undertaker Bert Denny asked me to look at them in case the sheriff wanted any information about them later. Your father was killed by a single shot which went right through his head. Your mother was drowned.'

'I heard that her head was bruised,' said Morgan.

'That's right,' said Garrett.

'Could she have been knocked unconscious and then dropped in the river?' asked Morgan. 'I know she couldn't swim.'

Garrett's jaw dropped and he stared at Morgan for a moment before replying.

'It could have happened like that,' he said, slowly. 'But who on earth would sink so low as to kill a defenceless woman in that way?'

'Maybe the same person who killed my father,' replied Morgan.

'You really think that?' asked Garrett.

'It's possible,' replied Morgan, 'but please

keep the idea to yourself for now, while I nose around.'

When Morgan left the doctor's house he figured it was time for him to ride out to the Crazy R. He decided to go there the following morning.

Four

The next day, as Morgan approached the Crazy R ranch buildings, he saw several hands occupied around them, and two men standing outside the house looking in his direction. He headed towards the house, glancing at a stocky, bearded man standing outside the bunkhouse as he passed close by him.

This man observed Morgan closely and continued to watch him as he rode up to the two men outside the ranch house and stopped in front of them.

Immediately, Morgan recognized Kennedy from his aunt's description. He spoke to the rancher.

'I reckon you're the owner of this ranch?' he said.

'I am,' replied Kennedy abruptly. 'What's

your business here?'

'I'm Morgan Cassidy,' said Morgan. 'I'd like a few words with you.'

'I'm glad you're here, Cassidy,' said Kennedy. 'I have something for you. Come inside.' He pointed to his companion, who was wearing a six-gun. 'This is my foreman, Wes Hartley.'

Morgan followed the two men inside and into the living-room. Kennedy walked over to a desk and took out a packet which he handed to Morgan.

'The money I paid your mother for the ranch,' he said. 'It's inside there. That's the same packet it was in when I handed it over to her. Wes here found it in the Box C ranch house when my men moved in. I've been holding it for you till you showed up.'

'I can't believe,' said Morgan, 'that my mother would sell the place without telling me beforehand.'

'I've no notion of what was in her mind,' said Kennedy. 'She seemed to know what she was doing at the time. But you can see the bill of sale if it'll make your mind easier.' There was a sharp edge to his voice.

He walked over to a desk and took out a document which he handed to Morgan. Reading it, Morgan could see that it appeared to be an authentic legal transfer of the Box C range, buildings and stock to Kennedy. His mother's signature, which appeared to be genuine, had been witnessed by Dawson the banker.

Morgan handed the document back to Kennedy.

'I hope you're satisfied now that everything's above-board,' said the rancher.

'You must be crazy, to think I'm satisfied, Kennedy,' said Morgan. 'I know my mother too well. My guess is that you're so greedy and hungry for land that you couldn't stand for a small ranch sitting in the middle of your range. I think it's very likely that you're responsible for the deaths of both my parents. My job now is to prove it.'

Kennedy's face purpled. Hartley's hand moved tentatively towards the handle of his six-gun and he glanced at the rancher. But both men froze as the long-barrelled Peacemaker appeared miraculously in Morgan's right hand, pointing towards the rancher.

Morgan took the foreman's gun out of its holster, then looked around the room.

'Just so's I can get away from here without getting shot in the back,' he said, 'you two had better step over there.' He pointed with his revolver towards the door of a small cupboard which had been built under the staircase.

Fuming, Kennedy walked up to the door, with Hartley by his side.

'You ain't going to get away with this, Cassidy,' he said. 'You're as good as dead right now.'

'Open that cupboard door,' ordered Morgan, 'and get inside, both of you.' He jabbed the muzzle of his six-gun into Kennedy's back.

His face contorted with rage, the rancher squeezed into the small amount of clear space left in the cupboard, and Hartley pushed in after him. There was barely room for them to move.

'I'm going to stay in the room here for a while,' said Morgan. 'I won't say for how long. But if I see the latch on this cupboard door moving, I'll send a bullet through the door. The way you're crammed in there, it's bound to hit one of you. And as soon as I get the proof that you had my parents killed, Kennedy, I'll be coming for you.'

He pushed the door to and engaged the latch. Then, with his knife, he cut a short, thin piece of wood from one of the logs standing near the stove, trimmed it to the right size, and jammed the latch with it so that the bar could not be lifted to open the door.

Then he pushed a heavy wooden chest standing to one side of the door into a position across it. He moved it as close to the door as possible, then left the ranch house, mounted his horse and headed for town.

It was almost twenty minutes before the

enraged rancher and his foreman succeeded in forcing their way out of the cupboard.

Morgan's aunt had told him that when Kennedy took over the Box C, his father's two hands Jardine and Clark had gone to the Triangle T ranch, about twenty miles north of Dennison. They had heard that the owner, Tanner, was short of hands.

Morgan changed his mind about riding into town and headed north for the Triangle T. He reached the spread in the afternoon and rode towards the ranch house, then veered towards a man who had just appeared in the doorway of the barn.

'I'm looking for Mr Tanner,' said Morgan.

'That's me,' said the man, a spry, pleasant looking individual in his forties.

Morgan introduced himself and explained his business.

'I was mighty sorry,' said Tanner, 'to hear from Jardine about the trouble you've had on the Box C. I met your father a couple of times. Clark and Jardine are both out on the range moving some cattle, but I'm expecting them back any time now. They're both good men.'

'Yes, I know,' said Morgan. 'They'd both been with my father for five years before they had to leave.'

'Come over to the house,' said Tanner. 'We'll wait there till they get here.'

The two men chatted until, half an hour later, Tanner, looking through a window, saw Jardine and Clark ride up. He suggested that Morgan go and talk with them in the bunkhouse.

The two hands, surprised to see Morgan, went into the bunkhouse with him. He questioned them closely about events during the period covering the deaths of his parents.

Some interesting facts emerged from the conversation. Jardine, who had found Walt Cassidy's body, mentioned that he had seen a Crazy R hand riding east out of town in the direction of the Crazy R and Box C ranches on the day of the ambush, just after he and Walt Cassidy arrived in town.

The man Jardine had seen leaving town was called Hendrick. He had arrived at the Crazy R Ranch a few weeks previously. He was, said Jardine, a mean-looking character, stocky and bearded, always carrying a six-gun. An old scar, very prominent, ran down his right temple, close to his eye, and disappeared under his beard.

He was a bit of a loner, going into town, unaccompanied, several times a week, to drink at the saloon.

'This man Hendrick,' said Morgan, 'I'm pretty sure I saw him at the Crazy R when I rode out there to see Kennedy.'

The two hands went on to tell Morgan that on the day Sarah Cassidy had been found dead in the river, she had seemed quite normal when they left her in mid-morning to doctor some cows for blowflies. She had mentioned that she was looking forward to Morgan's arrival.

But one thing had struck them as very unusual when they got back to the ranch house that day and found Sarah missing.

Her wide-brimmed hat, which she invariably wore outside in hot sunny weather such as they were having at the time, was still inside the house.

The hands further told Morgan that on the day before the death of his mother, they had both been out on the range and they weren't able to confirm Dawson's story that the banker and Kennedy had visited his mother at the ranch that day. But she had said nothing to them about the two men being there.

Morgan thanked the two hands, went to see Tanner for a few minutes, then rode back to Dennison, feeling more sure than ever that his mother had been murdered.

When he reached town he rode along to the livery stable and handed his horse over to Hal Jenkins. He told him of his visits to the Crazy R earlier in the day and to the ranch where Jardine and Clark were now working.

'This man Hendrick from the Crazy R that Jardine mentioned,' he said. 'D'you know him?'

'I've seen him in town fairly regular,' replied Jenkins, 'but he ain't been to the stable and I've never had words with him. I saw him go into the saloon today. He sure is a mean-looking *hombre.*'

The following morning Morgan rode out to the place where his father's body had been found. He walked into the grove and following Jardine's directions he soon found the place, just within the grove and behind the trunk of a tree, where the killer had waited to ambush his father. There were still signs of the ground being flattened where the killer had stood.

Morgan got down on his hands and knees and meticulously examined the ground around the base of the tree, inch by inch. He was just about to get up when his eye was caught by a small shred of brown material protruding from the ground.

Carefully, with the point of his knife, he loosened the soil around it and lifted from the ground the unsmoked end, about an inch long, of a cigarillo. It had obviously been pressed into the ground by the sole or heel of a boot. He stowed it carefully in his vest pocket, then rode back to the livery stable in town.

He showed Jenkins the cigarillo butt which he had found in the grove.

'I'm interested in finding out,' he said, 'whether that Crazy R man Hendrick smokes these. Who's the best person to ask?'

'That would be the barkeep in the saloon just along the street there,' replied Jenkins. 'It so happens he's my brother Jim. Hendrick spends a fair amount of time in there. I know Jim's off duty just now. He has a room over the saloon. Wait here, I'll go and get him.'

Ten minutes later Jenkins returned with his brother. Morgan showed the barkeep the butt and asked him if he had seen Hendrick smoking cigarillos of that type.

'I have,' replied the barkeep. 'In fact, he buys them from me now and again. Each time he comes in here he smokes maybe a couple.'

'Does anybody else smoke them that you know of?' asked Morgan.

'An old-timer called Bancroft buys a few now and again,' replied the barkeep, 'but he's eighty years old. And I smoke maybe one a day myself. Can't think of anybody else.'

'Thanks for the information,' said Morgan. 'I'd be obliged if you don't mention to anybody that I've been asking these questions.'

'You can count on it,' said the barkeep, and turned to leave. Then he paused. 'I guess you know,' he said, 'that Hendrick isn't going to be around for a while?'

'No, I didn't know that,' said Morgan.

'He called in around noon,' said the barkeep. 'He had a drink, then bought all the cigarillos I could spare. Said he was leaving the Crazy R for a spell. Didn't say where he was going or for how long.'

'I saw him leave,' said Hal Jenkins. 'He was riding along the main trail to the east. I kept my eye on him for a while. If he stays on that trail long enough it'll take him into Kansas. It runs pretty straight right up to the border. You figuring to go after him, Morgan?'

'I am,' replied Morgan. 'I'm near certain now that it was Hendrick who killed my father. I want to catch up with him before he gets too far. Kennedy can wait. What kind of a horse was Hendrick riding?'

'It was a big chestnut with a white blaze running down its face,' the liveryman replied. 'And Hendrick was wearing a black hat and black pants and vest.'

'I'm going to get on his trail right away,' said Morgan.

Five

Night had just fallen when Morgan set off. On the assumption that Hendrick, not expecting to be followed, would stay on the main trail to the east, he had decided to ride as fast as he could along it until well after midnight, when he would take a few hours' rest. Then he would carry on at first light, in the hope that he would eventually catch up with his quarry.

He spent the latter part of the night in a small hollow just off the trail and resumed his pursuit at dawn. It was after dark when he came to the small town of Enderby, where he had a stroke of luck. The storekeeper told him that a stranger answering Hendrick's description had called in the store about three hours earlier and had ridden off along the trail to the east. He was riding a big chestnut.

Morgan continued his pursuit, hoping that Hendrick would be camping out somewhere on the trail ahead and that he would come upon his camp sometime during the night.

It was around ten o'clock when he spotted a light ahead, just off the trail, to the left. It looked like the light from a camp-fire. He dismounted when he was about four hundred yards from the light and led his horse off the trail to a patch of brush, where he tied it to a small tree.

Uncertain about whether the camp-fire was Hendrick's he decided to find out. The ground between him and the fire was rough, dotted with large boulders. Using these for cover he moved towards the fire. He paused when he could see that there was not one man, but three, seated near the fire. He moved forward again, then froze as the faint sound of a lullaby drifted through the still night air.

The sound came from his left and he

started moving cautiously towards it. He was fairly certain that a herd of cows was bedded down somewhere in that direction, but he wanted to make sure. He stopped as he reached the lip of a large shallow basin.

He could see the dim shapes of cows lying on the ground, and two trail hands, one of them singing a lullaby to settle the cattle down. The two men were circling the herd in opposite directions.

Morgan's next task was to find out whether Hendrick was one of the men around the fire. He retraced his steps, circled the fire at a distance until it was between him and the herd, then moved as close as he could without being seen, to the fire and the three men seated close to it.

Crouching behind a large boulder he studied the men closely. One of them looked like a half-breed and the one sitting close to him was too slim and tall to be Hendrick. The third, a man dressed in black clothing, was the right build but his back was to Morgan. Then, as he turned his head,

Morgan saw his face and knew that he had caught up with the man who had murdered his father.

As he watched the three men he wondered whether Hendrick had come purposely to meet the others or whether they were strangers and he was just camping with them overnight for company.

He decided to stay where he was until the men turned in, after which he might be able to work out some way of capturing Hendrick. He could hear the murmur of their voices, but was too far away to make out what they were saying.

Thirty-five minutes had passed when the half-breed rose to his feet, exchanged a few words with the tall man, then walked off in the direction of the herd. He quickly disappeared into the darkness.

Morgan felt uneasy at the absence of the half-breed, but reasoned that he had probably gone to the herd to relieve one of the night guards, who would be appearing soon. But twenty minutes passed and no one returned.

Increasingly nervous Morgan decided to withdraw from the camp for the time being and he started to turn. As he did so, the half-breed, moving soundlessly in on him, jammed the muzzle of a six-gun against the side of his neck.

'Move, and you're a dead man,' he said.

Morgan froze, and the 'breed, a half-Comanche called Porter, lifted his prisoner's gun from its holster. Then, prodding Morgan in the back with the muzzle of his revolver, he ordered him to walk towards the two men near the fire. He called out to them that he was bringing a prisoner in.

The two men rose hastily to their feet, curious as to the identity of the man walking towards them with Porter close behind him. Soon they were able to see his face in the light from the fire. He stopped in front of them.

'Well, I'm damned!' said Hendrick, turning to the tall man, whose name was Butler. 'This is the man Cassidy I've just been talking about. He's the one Kennedy was aiming to kill before you drove the herd on to the ranch.

'Like I told you, he didn't want to risk Cassidy here seeing the cattle you're bringing in because until his men do some work on the brands, it's clear that it's a herd of rustled cows. So he sent me along to tell you to hold the herd here for the time being.'

'Well,' said Butler, 'now that we've got him, can we carry on with the drive?'

'I guess so,' replied Hendrick. 'The question is, what do we do with Cassidy? I'm wondering if he followed me because he got the idea that I bushwhacked his father.' He turned to Morgan. 'Was that the reason, Cassidy? If it was, I can tell you now that you guessed right. Your father should have had the sense to sell out to Kennedy.'

'I figured it was you, Hendrick,' said Morgan, forcing himself to speak calmly, 'and I expect you had a hand in my mother's death as well.'

'Not guilty,' said Hendrick. 'Since you

ain't got long to live I don't see no harm in letting you know that Kennedy tended to that personally, with Hartley lending a hand. The way I heard it was that when your mother told Kennedy again at the ranch that she wasn't going to sell, they knocked her out with a punch to the head and dropped her in the river.

'Then they pulled her out and made out they'd found her body in the river a few miles downstream on Crazy R range. Once she was out of the way, all that Kennedy and that banker Dawson had to do was fake the bill of sale. Like I said before, your father should have sold out while he had the chance.'

With a supreme effort Morgan suppressed an almost overpowering impulse to rush forward and get his hands on Hendrick, despite the gun at his back. He stayed silent.

'It's a good thing you sent me out to scout around the camp,' said Porter to Butler. 'I found Cassidy's horse first. Then I started looking for him. I found him watching you from behind that boulder over there.'

'I'm a cautious man,' said Butler, 'especially when I'm driving a herd of rustled cattle. Better tie him up.'

He held a gun on Morgan while Porter ordered the prisoner to sit on the ground, then tied him hand and foot. Then Butler drew Hendrick aside, out of earshot of Morgan.

'What do we do with this man?' he asked.

'We finish him off, of course,' replied Hendrick. 'Kennedy's going to be mighty pleased when he hears that Cassidy ain't around no more. Might even feel like giving us a bonus.'

'We do it right now?' asked Butler.

Hendrick thought for a moment before he replied. 'I don't think so,' he said. 'I heard that Cassidy's a deputy US marshal in Indian Territory. We've got to make his death look like an accident, if we don't want the law snooping around.'

They continued discussing the disposal of Morgan for a while, then returned to Porter.

Morgan suspected that they had been deciding his fate. His death was probably only a matter of a few minutes or hours away.

He heard Butler ask Hendrick if he was staying on at the Crazy R when they arrived there.

'I'll be leaving as soon as I can,' said Hendrick. 'Kennedy wants me to stay on but my brother-in-law Herb Kitchen is planning a bank robbery in Caldwell, Kansas, in about two months time, and he wants me to join him. He's hiding out near there.'

He yawned. 'Reckon I'll turn in now,' he said. 'It's been a long day.'

Morgan spent an uncomfortable night, still bound and lying near the fire. His arms and legs were so tightly held by the ropes around them that there was no chance of freeing himself or crawling away un-observed.

At midnight the two men Butler and Porter went out to the herd to relieve the two hands Russell and Carver, and they changed over again around four in the morning.

They put the cows on the trail soon after daylight. Morgan, who was not given breakfast, was ordered to mount his own horse. His hands were then tied behind him and his horse was led by Hendrick, riding slightly in front of him and to one side. Porter was riding to the left of Hendrick, on the right flank of the moving line of cows.

About three hours into the day's drive, they reached a point where the cattle were moving parallel to a deep canyon on the right. Morgan had noticed this as he passed by in the dark on the previous evening, but he had no idea of its depth.

Butler, who had been riding just ahead of the herd, rode back to Hendrick and the two men turned and rode towards the top of the canyon wall. Hendrick was still leading Morgan's horse behind him. They came to a halt a few yards back from the edge and both men dismounted.

Butler held the reins of Morgan's horse while Hendrick walked a few paces forward and looked down into the canyon. For the first thirty yards or so there was a fairly steep slope. Its surface was of smooth rock interspersed with some areas which were covered with earth and small stones and a scattering of small buried rocks protruding above the surface. Here and there a short sturdy-looking shrub had taken root.

The slope gave way abruptly to an almost sheer drop to the hard dry floor of the canyon well over a hundred feet below.

Hendrick turned, nodded to Butler, and started to walk back towards him. Butler reached up and behind Morgan to grab his tied hands, and pulled him out of the saddle. As he hit the ground Hendrick struck him over the head with the barrel of his Colt.

When Morgan lay on the ground, stunned, Hendrick quickly slashed through the ropes around his wrists, dragged him to the canyon rim, and rolled him over the edge. Then, seeing that Butler was having difficulty controlling Morgan's horse, startled by the sudden loss of its rider, he ran to help him.

Unconscious, Morgan rolled and slid down the slope, gaining speed as he went. A third of the way down to the sheer wall his left shoulder struck a protruding rock. His body slewed round, and a moment later rolled over a long low rocky projection. As he did so, his left foot caught in a crevice in the rock, and his fall was momentarily checked until the foot came free. It was at this point that Morgan started to come round.

Directly beneath him on the slope, and only two feet from the sheer drop to the canyon floor, was a sturdy shrub, four feet tall, with a stout trunk. It was rooted in a crevice in the rocky incline. Its foliage stretched almost down to the surface of the slope.

Morgan's chest slammed into the trunk. His body slewed and started sliding towards the sheer drop only two feet away. As he became fully conscious, he twisted, and grabbed the trunk with both hands.

When he came to rest, the lower half of his body was hanging down over the top edge of the canyon wall. The upper part of his body was screened from the view of anyone looking down from directly above him by the foliage growing from the trunk he was desperately hanging on to.

Up above him, Hendrick and Butler manoeuvred Morgan's horse so that it was facing away from the canyon, with its hind feet not far from the edge. Then Hendrick fired off his six-gun only inches away from the horse's face.

The frightened animal reared and moved backwards as the two men released it. Its hind feet dropped over the edge and started to slide downwards. Frantically, it tried to scramble upwards, but as Hendrick and Butler pushed hard against its chest its forefeet went over the edge. The animal fell on its side and slid down the slope.

The two men watched, as the horse, squealing in terror, tried vainly to regain its feet before it reached the sheer drop and disappeared from view. They stood for a short while, looking down the slope.

'Well,' said Hendrick, 'that's the end of Cassidy. And if anybody comes across him and his horse, there ain't nothing to show that it wasn't an accident.'

'Ain't you going to find a way into the canyon, so's you can make sure he's dead?' asked Butler.

'That could take quite a long while,' replied Hendrick, 'and I reckon it would be a waste of time. Nobody could fall that far and stay alive.'

Butler looked down at the floor of the canyon, visible on the far side. 'I guess you're right,' he said.

Hanging desperately on to the trunk, Morgan saw his horse slide past him, its legs thrashing wildly. It missed the tree by inches, and disappeared over the edge. Moments later, he heard the sound of voices above him. Then there was silence.

The pain in his shoulder was so intense that he had to fight off an attack of faintness which threatened to loosen his grip on the trunk and send him plummeting to his death far below.

Groaning with pain he managed to pull himself upwards so that he could place his right knee on the slope below the tree. Then, still holding on to the trunk, he crawled up to it and around it, and lay down in such a position that the trunk prevented his body from sliding further down the slope.

There, he tried to assess his injuries. He was fairly sure that his left shoulder was dislocated and that his right ankle had been sprained. Also, he suspected that one or more of his ribs had been damaged.

He looked up the slope, wondering what his chances were of being able to climb to the top, handicapped as he was, without losing his grip and falling to certain death below. Rating them about even, he started to make his way upwards. He chose a zigzag path which looked like providing reasonably firm handholds and footholds to take him up the slope to the top. Slowly he worked his way upwards, doing his best to ignore the pain in his left arm and shoulder, his ankle and his ribs.

Frequently he stopped to rest and it was well over an hour before he reached the top of the slope, his face beaded with sweat and his body racked with pain. He lay still for half an hour to allow the pain to subside a little. There was no sign of Butler and Hendrick, or of the trail herd.

He knew that he needed a doctor's attention and decided that he would head for Enderby, the town he had passed through the previous evening. He judged that it was about four miles distant.

Putting his weight on his right leg, he got to his feet and attempted to walk. He found that he could put very little weight on his left ankle and that any body movement increased the pain in the rib area.

He started limping painfully – and slowly – towards Enderby. After he had covered a quarter of a mile he came to a small group of trees by the trail and broke off a branch which would serve as a walking-stick and take some of the weight off his injured ankle.

He carried on, a little more quickly than before, but was forced to rest now and again when the pain became intolerable. During one of these rest periods he saw a buggy on his left, moving along a side track which joined up with the main trail he himself was following, just a little way ahead.

He stood up and waved to the buggy and saw the man inside wave back. The buggy continued on until it reached the main trail, then turned and headed towards Morgan. He waited until it reached him and stopped.

There was one man inside. He was middle-aged and dressed in a dark suit and hat. By his side, on the seat was a large black bag. Morgan looked at the man, then at the bag.

'I've got a feeling,' he said, 'that maybe I'm in luck. You wouldn't be a doctor, would you?'

The man in the buggy smiled. 'I sure am,' he said. 'My name's Carpenter, from Enderby. You in trouble?'

'You could say that,' replied Morgan. 'I'm pretty sure that my shoulder's out of joint, my right ankle ain't working too good, and it feels like I have one or two busted ribs.'

'I sure am curious to hear how you got in such a state,' said Carpenter, 'but that can wait.'

He climbed down from the buggy. 'Let's have a look at the shoulder first,' he said.

He examined it carefully. 'It's dislocated all right,' he told Morgan, when he had finished. 'I'm going to put the joint back like it should be. But I warn you, it's really going to hurt.'

He manoeuvred Morgan's left arm so that the elbow was over the chest. Then he pulled the forearm down and rotated the arm. The procedure was so painful that

Morgan yelled out involuntarily and was near to fainting.

'That's done it,' said Carpenter, 'but it'll be a while before it's really back to normal again.'

He took a quick look at Morgan's chest and ankle and bandaged them both.

'That'll do till we get back to my house,' he said. 'I'll have a closer look at them there.'

He helped Morgan up on to the seat of the buggy and climbed up beside him. As they drove towards the town Morgan told the doctor about the death of his parents, and how he had come by his present injuries.

Carpenter was shocked. 'I saw that trail herd passing by when I left town this morning,' he said. 'This man Kennedy sounds like a real villain. How d'you reckon you're going to bring him to book? It looks too big a job for one man on his own.'

'I'll work out a plan,' replied Morgan. 'Kennedy and his foreman and Hendrick have all got to be made to pay for what they done to my parents and me. I'm going after them as soon as I can.'

'It'll be a while,' said the doctor, 'before you're well enough to start out on a job like that. You're welcome to stay at my place till you're fit again.'

'I'm mighty obliged to you for the offer,' said Morgan, 'and I'm going to take you up on it. I've got no money on me now, but as soon as I get back to Dennison I'll send you money for my treatment and keep.'

'There's no hurry,' said Carpenter. 'Any time'll do. I figure you're a man I can trust.'

'What I've just told you about myself,' said Morgan, 'I'd be obliged if you don't repeat it to anybody in Enderby. I don't want to risk Kennedy hearing that I'm still alive. With him thinking I'm dead, I've got a better chance of bringing him down.'

'You're right,' said the doctor. 'I'll put the story around that your horse took a bad fall and rolled over you, and you had to shoot it. I'll say I came across you out on the trail soon after it happened.'

When they reached town Morgan followed Carpenter into his house and the doctor carried out a thorough examination of his chest and ankle.

'As far as I can tell,' he said, when he had finished, 'the ankle's sprained, not fractured, and you've got a broken rib. This means that you've got to rest up for several weeks before you'll be fit enough to go after Kennedy and the others. I've got a small room with a bed you can use. When I've bandaged you up you can go in there and rest.'

Six

For the next five weeks Morgan stayed at the doctor's house. During the last week he did some riding, after which Carpenter told him he was fit to travel and wished him well.

Before leaving for Dennison Morgan thanked the doctor and told him that he would send the money for his treatment and keep, and for a horse and a six-gun and belt which Carpenter had bought for him in town.

He camped out overnight, and setting off after breakfast, he maintained a pace which brought him into Dennison around nine o'clock in the evening. He rode along the street, keeping in the shadows, and tied his horse to a hitching rail outside the livery stable.

He walked along the side of the stable,

then on to the door of the liveryman's house. He could see that there was a light on inside. He knocked on the door, which was opened shortly after by Hal Jenkins. It was a moment before the liveryman recognized Morgan. When he did, he quickly grabbed his arm and pulled him inside.

'When I saw Hendrick in town a few days after you left here on his trail,' he said, 'I started wondering whether you'd run into trouble. And when you didn't turn up in the next few weeks I was sure you had. And Betty Burke's been some worried as well. What in tarnation happened to you?'

Morgan told Jenkins about his capture by Hendrick and the rustlers, followed by his escape.

'I don't want Kennedy to know I'm still alive,' he said. 'So I don't want anybody in town, except you and my aunt, to know that I'm back. I'll hide out somewhere while I think up some way of dealing with Kennedy and the others.'

'I've got a spare room here with a bed inside,' said Jenkins. 'You can use that. I'll put your horse in the stable. And you can be sure I'll keep quiet about your being here.'

'I'm much obliged,' said Morgan. 'Is Hendrick still around?'

'Hendrick has gone,' replied Jenkins. 'He told my brother Jim, the barkeep, about four weeks ago, that he was leaving, and we ain't seen him in town since.'

'I have a good idea where he's gone,' said Morgan. 'Anything interesting happened around here since I left?'

'Just after noon today,' said Jenkins, 'a rider came into town and asked me for directions to the Cassidy ranch. I told him it had changed hands and he asked if you were around. Said he was a friend of yours. Didn't give his name.

'I told him that you'd ridden off a while ago and I didn't know when you were coming back. He left his horse here and went to the hotel. Said he was aiming to stay here overnight.'

'That is interesting,' said Morgan. 'What did this man look like?'

'The thing I noticed most about him,' replied Jenkins, 'was his hair. Brightest red I've ever seen. Apart from that I reckon he was about your age and size. And one other thing, I noticed he walked with a slight limp.'

'Johnny Trimble!' said Morgan. 'Couldn't be anybody else. But what in blazes is he doing here in Dennison, I wonder?

'Johnny,' he explained to Jenkins, 'was my friend and partner for a year when we were both working as deputies in Indian Territory. About a year ago we split up when he was posted to another part of the Territory. They don't come any better than Johnny.'

'Would you like me to go over to the hotel,' enquired Jenkins, 'and ask him to come over to see you?'

'I sure would,' replied Morgan. 'I'm mighty curious to find out why he's here. And while you're out, would you mind telling Betty Burke that I'm back. Tell her

I'll drop in to see her later, and say I don't want anybody else in town to know I'm here. Say I'll explain everything when I see her.'

'I'll do that,' said Jenkins.

He was back twenty minutes later with Johnny Trimble. Morgan greeted his friend and all three sat down in the living-room.

'I've been wondering, Johnny,' said Morgan, 'just what brings you here.'

'I quit my job a week ago,' said Johnny. 'Felt I needed a change. Just before I left I heard from the US marshal in Fort Smith that you'd taken leave to look into the murder of your father. So I hightailed it here. Thought maybe I could help.'

'I sure am glad you turned up,' said Morgan. 'Did you tell anybody else, apart from Hal here, that you were looking for me?'

'No, I didn't,' replied Johnny.

'We'd best leave it like that, then,' said Morgan, and went on to tell his friend all that had happened since he first heard from his mother about his father's murder.

'This man Kennedy,' said Johnny when Morgan had finished, 'it's clear he's got to be stopped. You got a plan, Morgan?'

'I've been working on one,' replied Morgan, 'but I'm going to start on a better one now that you're here. How long can you stay?'

'As long as it takes,' Johnny replied. 'My folks in Julesberg are expecting me to turn up there soon, but I'll telegraph them in the morning to say I'm staying on here for a spell.'

'I sure do appreciate you offering to help me out like this,' said Morgan. 'It could be a dangerous business. Now that I've had it from Hendrick's own mouth that he killed my father and that Kennedy and Hartley were responsible for my mother's death, I suppose I could send a message to the US marshal in Denver. But I don't know how long it would take him to get somebody here, and I'm going to get a lot more personal satisfaction out of it if I take a hand myself.

'What I'm aiming to do is capture Kennedy and his foreman Hartley, and Dawson the banker, and take them to the US marshal in Denver. According to Hendrick, after my mother had been killed Dawson drew up a fake bill of sale showing Kennedy as the new owner of the Box C.'

'How about Hendrick?' asked Jenkins.

'He'll have to wait till we've finished our job here,' Morgan replied. 'For the time being I want to concentrate on the other three. Have you any idea how many men Kennedy has at the ranch just now?'

'I'm guessing,' replied Jenkins, 'but there must be around ten, outside of the foreman, mostly hard-looking cases, wearing guns.'

'It's clear, then,' said Morgan, 'that we can't just ride up to the Crazy R in broad daylight and expect to capture Kennedy and Hartley without any trouble. Lead would start flying as soon as I was recognized.'

He turned to Jenkins. 'It might turn out,' he said, 'that the need crops up for a hiding-place in town where Kennedy's men couldn't find us if they made a search of the buildings. Can you think of anywhere we could go?'

The liveryman pondered only briefly before he replied. 'I know just the place,' he said. 'It's in the stable loft. There's a false wall up there, with a three-foot space between it and the real wall. Just why it was built like that by the man who ran the stable before me, I can't say. I use it myself as a small store, but I can soon clear it out.

'There's a door leads into it, but I've got some planks up there I could use to stack up against that. With the door hidden, no stranger would guess that there was a space behind that wall. I'll clear it out in the morning.'

'Thanks,' said Morgan. 'That sounds just right, and I appreciate the offer.'

'I just had an idea,' said Johnny. 'How about me riding out to the Crazy R, casual-like, and asking for a job? If I managed to get on the payroll, I could have a good look at the situation out there, and maybe we could work out a plan to take Kennedy and his foreman without a lot of gunplay.'

'Sounds good to me,' said Morgan, 'if you're willing to take the risk.'

'I am,' said Johnny.

'In that case,' said Morgan, 'we'll take Kennedy and Hartley first and hold them somewhere while I go after the banker.'

'I'll ride out to the ranch early in the morning,' said Johnny, 'and if I'm taken on, I'll get a message to you through Hal here as soon as I can think up a plan for getting hold of Kennedy and his foreman. You'll be staying inside, Morgan, out of sight, I reckon?'

'I will,' said Morgan, 'apart from sneaking out to have a few words with Aunt Betty. Now, let me give you some information that might help you to persuade Kennedy to take you on.'

Fifteen minutes later, Johnny left for the hotel and shortly after, Morgan followed him out and walked to the general store, making sure he wasn't observed. Almost immediately his aunt answered his knock on the back door and ushered him into the living-room.

'I've been worried sick,' she said. 'Couldn't help but think the worst when you didn't come back.'

Morgan explained his absence, and told her that he now knew that Hendrick had murdered his father and that his mother had been killed by Kennedy and his foreman. He also told her of Johnny's arrival in town and said that they planned to hand Kennedy and Hartley over to the law, together with Dawson.

'I'm hiding out at the livery stable for the time being,' he said before leaving, 'and Johnny's going to see if he can get a job at the Crazy R. We'll let you know how things pan out.'

First thing the following morning Morgan prepared a message to the town marshal at Caldwell, Kansas, advising him that he had grounds to believe that a criminal called Ty Hendrick and his brother-in-law Herb

Kitchen were planning a bank robbery in Caldwell in the near future. He signed the message: 'Morgan Cassidy, deputy US marshal, Indian Territory.'

He gave the message to Jenkins, who said he would hand it in at the telegraph office.

'The operator won't talk,' he assured Morgan. 'He's a friend of mine.'

Just before noon, Johnny approached the Crazy R ranch house. Several hands were moving around, and he paused to check with a man outside the barn whether Kennedy was in the house. The man nodded and Johnny rode up to the house, dismounted, and knocked on the door. It was opened by a middle-aged Mexican woman holding a duster in her hand. Before she could speak a man appeared behind her, pushed her aside, and she disappeared inside the house. The man now standing in front of Johnny tallied with Morgan's description of the rancher.

'Mr Kennedy?' asked Johnny.

The rancher nodded. 'What do you want?'

he asked abruptly.

'My name's Trimble,' said Johnny. 'I'm looking for work. You need a good hand?'

'No, I don't,' said Kennedy, tersely. 'You wasted your time riding out here.'

Johnny turned and started moving towards his horse. 'Looks like I got the wrong idea from Hendrick,' he said. 'He reckoned you'd take me on.'

Kennedy, who had turned to go back into the house, swung round and called out after Johnny.

'You know Hendrick?' he asked.

Johnny stopped and turned to face him. 'Sure,' he replied. 'We've worked together a couple of times in the past. Last time I saw him was in Kansas a few weeks ago.'

'That's when he told you about me?' asked Kennedy.

'That's right,' said Johnny. 'Dunno if he told you, but he was joining up with his brother-in-law's gang to rob a bank in Caldwell. I asked him if they needed an extra man, but he said they didn't. That's when he mentioned you.

'He told me how you got hold of the Cassidy ranch and how he got rid of Morgan Cassidy for you in that canyon. I could tell he really admired the way you worked.'

'Seems to me,' said Kennedy, grimly, 'that Hendrick has a weakness for shooting off his mouth.'

'It was between friends,' said Johnny. 'He knew it wouldn't go no further.'

Kennedy looked searchingly at Johnny before he spoke again.

'I'm going to need another good man soon,' he said. 'Not for punching cows – I've got plenty who can do that – but for a couple of jobs that ain't exactly legal. Are you interested?'

'I am,' replied Johnny, 'so long as the pay's good.'

'I reckon we can agree on the pay,' said Kennedy.

When they had done this, the rancher pointed to a small shack next to the bunkhouse. 'You can use that,' he said. 'There's a bunk in there. I'll tell my foreman Wes Hartley about you when he rides in from the range later. And I'll talk about the jobs I want you to do when I have a plan worked out in my mind.

'Meantime, I'm expecting a small trail herd to arrive here tomorrow or the day after.'

'I aim to ride into town tomorrow morning,' said Johnny. 'I need to buy a few things from the store.'

Kennedy grunted assent and went back into the house.

Johnny went for a meal in the cookshack, introducing himself to the cook and the four hands already in there. After the meal, he wandered casually around the buildings for a while, then went into his shack and stayed there, lying on his bunk, until the cook beat out the signal for supper on his triangle.

There were now ten men seated at the long table in the cookshack. As Johnny walked in, he asked the cook if the ramrod was one of them.

'No,' replied the cook. 'He ain't back yet. In any case, he eats and sleeps at the house.'

Over the meal, Johnny surreptitiously studied his table companions. They looked a hard-bitten lot, some more so than others, and Johnny guessed that they were all aware of Kennedy's illegal activities.

After supper Johnny returned to his shack. As he did so, he noticed the Mexican woman he had seen in the house earlier. She was going into a small shack near to the house, accompanied by a Mexican man.

An hour later there was a knock on the door which he answered. Hartley, the ram-rod, stood outside. He walked in and looked hard at Johnny.

'I'm Hartley,' he said. 'Mr Kennedy told me about him taking you on. From now on you'll be taking your orders from me. You'll probably be in action a couple of days from now. I'm taking it for granted you're pretty good at handling a sidearm.'

'I ain't had no complaints on that score,' said Johnny. 'Well above average, I'd say.'

'Right,' said Hartley. 'Rest up while you can.' He turned abruptly and left the shack.

In the early hours of the morning Johnny slipped out of the shack. The sky was overcast. He moved slowly and noiselessly around all the buildings until he was sure that no guards had been posted against possible intruders. It seemed that Kennedy was not expecting any interference with his activities. Johnny returned to his shack and slept soundly until dawn.

After breakfast he spent a little while in his shack writing a short message to Morgan. He pocketed this, then went out for his horse, saddled it, and rode into town. As far as he knew, there were no Crazy R hands there.

He rode up to the livery stable, outside which Hal Jenkins was standing, looking in his direction. Johnny stopped close to the liveryman, who, unseen by anyone around, plucked a folded sheet of paper from Johnny's outstretched hand and transferred it to his own pocket.

'For Morgan,' said Johnny.

Jenkins nodded, and pointed along the street as if giving Johnny some directions. Johnny raised his arm and rode along to the saloon, where he had a beer.

The liveryman took the message into Morgan, who read it with interest and showed it to Jenkins. He discussed with the liveryman some items which he would need from him for the forthcoming operation.

Seven

Johnny took a meal in town at the small restaurant next to the hotel and arrived back at the Crazy R in mid-afternoon. He had a stroll around the buildings, familiarizing himself with the layout of the place, then went to his shack and lay on the bunk for a while.

Hearing voices outside, he rose and walked over to the window. Three riders passed by, all unfamiliar to him. He wondered if the trail herd had arrived.

At supper time, when Johnny sat down at the table in the cookshack, the three men he had seen riding by earlier were not yet present. They walked up to the cookshack a few minutes later. One of them, a man called Larsen, glanced through a window of the cookshack as they approached the door, and suddenly halted. Then he turned to his companions.

'You two carry on,' he said. 'I'll be with you soon.'

He walked quickly to the house and hammered on the door. It was opened by the Mexican woman.

'I have to see Mr Kennedy,' he said. 'Pronto.'

She hesitated, then showed him into the room where Kennedy and his foreman were seated at a small table eating supper. They looked up as Larsen entered. Kennedy scowled at the interruption.

'Thought you'd like to know,' said Larsen, hurriedly, before Kennedy could speak, 'you've got a lawman – or maybe he's an ex-lawman – taking supper right now in the cookshack. He's a red-headed man called Trimble.'

The rancher and Hartley both jumped to their feet.

'You sure about this?' asked Kennedy.

'Plumb sure,' replied Larsen. 'About a

year ago I watched him arrest a man for horse-stealing in a small town in Indian Territory. He was a deputy US marshal, working out of Fort Smith.'

'Does he know you?' asked Kennedy.

'No,' replied Larsen, 'and I'm sure he doesn't know he's been spotted. I saw him through the cookshack window and came right here to tell you.'

'He can't be working for the US marshal at Fort Smith now,' said Hartley. 'We're way out of Indian Territory here.'

'I suppose it's just possible,' said Kennedy, 'that he's working on his own to find out what happened to Cassidy. Maybe he's a friend of Cassidy's. Whatever the reason for him being here, we've got to beat it out of him. He sure fooled me with that story about being a friend of Hendrick's.

'Which raises another question. How did he come to know how we got hold of the Box C and how we got rid of Morgan Cassidy?'

'Should we go for him now?' asked Hartley.

'Yes,' replied Kennedy. 'We'll grab him before he's finished his supper. Then we'll take him along to the barn to knock the truth out of him.'

Johnny didn't stand a chance. Before he realized what was happening, the rancher had walked into the cookshack with Hartley and Larsen and the muzzles of two six-guns were jammed against his back while his own revolver was removed from its holster. He sat still, his hands resting on the top of the table. The other men taking supper stared at Johnny and the three men standing behind him.

'We've got a lawman here, men,' said Kennedy. 'Leastways he *was* a lawman in Indian Territory a year ago. I've got to find out what he's doing here, claiming that he's worked with Hendrick.'

He ordered two of his men, Barlow and Ford, to take the prisoner to the barn. He and the ramrod followed close behind, with drawn guns. Inside the barn, Kennedy told the two hands to tie Johnny, in a standing position, to a stout post which was helping to support the floor of the loft.

Kennedy and Hartley stood facing the prisoner, a few feet away from him. Anger was boiling up inside the rancher.

'We happen to know, Trimble,' he said, 'that a year ago you were a deputy marshal in Indian Territory. You've just been recognized by one of the men who brought a trail herd in today. So the story you told me about knowing Hendrick is a pack of lies.

'What I want to know is why you're here, whether you're still a lawman, and how is it you seem to know so much about what's been happening around here lately? You can tell me straight out or we can do it the hard way. Which is it going to be?'

'You'll get nothing out of me, Kennedy,' said Johnny, 'and let me tell you that whatever happens to me your rustling and killing days will soon be over.'

Kennedy's face reddened. He spoke to Barlow and Ford, both tough-looking characters with a strong dislike for lawmen.

'You two,' he said. 'See if you can change Trimble's mind for him. Take it in turns. But take care you don't finish him off before he tells us what we want to know. Start on the head. See if you can spoil those good looks of his a little.'

He turned to Johnny. 'Sing out, Trimble,' he said, 'just as soon as you're ready to talk.'

Barlow approached Johnny, whose arms were tied to his sides, and started slapping him hard on both sides of his face. After repeated blows, blood started to flow from one of the victim's nostrils. Barlow suspended his attack, but the prisoner showed no sign of wanting to speak.

'Let me have a go,' said Ford, impatiently, and Barlow made way for him.

Ford rained some full-blooded punches on the left side of his victim's jaw. Johnny was able to ride them to some degree, but they did considerable damage to his face. Then his attacker moved around a little and applied an uppercut to Johnny's jaw which slammed the back of his head against the solid post behind it.

Johnny lost consciousness and his head slumped forward. Ford raised his fist to hit him again.

'Stop!' shouted Kennedy. 'That's enough. Can't you see he's passed out? I don't want him dead. I want him talking. That was a damn fool punch to throw.'

Johnny came to as the rancher finished speaking. Kennedy looked at him.

'We'll leave him like this till daylight,' he said. 'Maybe, in the morning, he'll feel more like talking. If not, we'll think up some other way of opening his mouth.'

'We'd better have guards out overnight, I reckon,' said Hartley.

'You reckon right,' said Kennedy. 'Maybe Trimble has somebody working with him. Put two men outside the house and one outside the barn. And make sure Trimble's tied fast to that post. Better change the guards every four hours. Tell them to stay exactly where they're stationed and fire their hand-guns if they want help.'

Johnny's bonds were checked and tightened by Barlow. Then the four men left the barn, closing the door behind them, and leaving a lighted lamp standing on the floor not far from Johnny.

The prisoner felt weak and dizzy from the beating he had received, particularly from the last punch, and blood was pouring down his face on to his shoulder.

At a quarter to nine Barlow returned to take up his post as guard. He walked up to Johnny and once again checked the ropes holding him to the post. Then he left the barn, closed the door behind him, and stood with his back to it. He lit a cigarette and prepared for a four-hour vigil.

At exactly midnight, Morgan, leading three saddled horses, rode quietly up to the south-east corner of the Crazy R pasture fence and tied the horses to it. It was a dark night and the outlines of the ranch buildings were barely visible to him as he stood looking in their direction.

After five minutes had passed, then ten, he was distinctly worried. The proposals in Johnny's message to him had been quite clear. Johnny would meet him, at exactly midnight, at the place where Morgan was now standing.

Then they would go to the ranch house, where Kennedy and Hartley would be sleeping. They would take the two men, at gunpoint, to the horses, and would start on the journey to Denver, a hundred miles distant, to hand them over to the US marshal there.

It was, thought Morgan, a plan which had a good chance of success. With luck, the two men would not be missed until breakfast. By then they would be well on their way to Denver, with no chance of the Crazy R hands catching up with them. Dawson could be attended to later.

But something must have gone wrong. He waited another fifteen minutes, then decided to investigate. To be on the safe side he would assume that guards had been posted.

Leaving the horses securely tied to the fence, he started moving slowly towards the house in a crouching position, watching out and listening for any signs of movement. He stopped abruptly as he saw a match flare up briefly, ahead of him and slightly to his right, close to the barn.

It seemed that a guard had been posted outside the barn and he suspected that others might have been posted elsewhere. It was obvious that he would have to move with great care. He changed direction and circled round so that he was approaching the side of the barn remote from the house. As he drew closer he dropped to the ground and crawled forward, taking advantage of all available cover. From time to time he could see the glowing end of the guard's cigarette.

Eventually, he reached the side of the barn without being seen, and rose to his feet. Moving to the corner he peered round it, and could see the dim shape of Barlow, standing with his back to the door. It was clear that there was someone or something of value to Kennedy inside the barn. It was possible, Morgan thought, that Johnny was a prisoner there.

He drew back and froze as he heard the sound of the relief guard Ford approaching from the direction of the bunkhouse. The sound of their subsequent conversation was clearly audible to Morgan.

'How's Trimble?' asked Ford.

'Let's take a look,' replied Barlow and the two men went inside the barn. Johnny, sagging against the post, looked up at them as they approached him. Morgan tiptoed to one side of the open door and stood there listening.

'Don't look too good, does he?' said Barlow. 'You sure did a good job on his face.'

'I'm looking forward to a bit more of the same in the morning,' said Ford.

He checked the ropes around Johnny and both men left the barn just after Morgan had slid round the corner out of sight.

'Who's relieving you?' asked Barlow as he

was moving off towards the bunkhouse.

'It'll be Jones,' replied Ford, 'in four hours from now.'

Morgan waited until the sounds of Barlow's departure had died away. Then he peered round the corner of the barn at Ford. The guard was standing a few feet from the door with his back to it, looking straight in front of him.

From his pocket Morgan took a couple of small stones which he had picked up earlier and lobbed one over Ford's head to drop near the far corner of the barn. The sound it made was clearly audible in the still night air.

Ford turned to look in the direction of the sound. He drew his gun, then stood motionless. Morgan lobbed the second stone, a larger one this time, to land in the same place. As Ford started moving cautiously towards the sound, Morgan moved up noiselessly behind him and struck the guard hard on the back of the head with the barrel of his revolver.

Ford stumbled forward, dropping his gun, then fell to the ground and lay motionless. Morgan opened the barn door sufficiently to allow him to drag the guard inside, then closed it behind him. Johnny viewed the proceedings with considerable relief.

Morgan tied Ford's bandanna over his eyes, then, using his own bandanna, he gagged the guard. Ford still lay motionless as Morgan walked over to Johnny and looked with concern at the battered face of his friend. Hurriedly, he undid the ropes binding Johnny to the post and the ones around his wrists and ankles.

'I've been expecting you,' said Johnny.

'You able to ride?' asked Morgan.

'Sure,' replied his friend. 'I've got a pretty sore head, but the rest of me is all right.'

He looked at Ford. 'There's the one that did most of the damage,' he said. 'Glad to see that he's had a taste of his own medicine.'

As Morgan finished untying his friend, Ford stirred. Morgan used the rope to bind the arms and legs of the Crazy R hand, and to secure him to the same post that Johnny had been fastened to. He was sure, when he had finished, that the bound man would not be able to free himself unaided. The blindfolded guard, cursing feebly, was unable to see the man who had attacked him.

Johnny flexed his legs to restore the circulation, then he and Morgan left the barn, closing the door behind them.

'With luck,' said Morgan, 'we've got a little under four hours to get settled in that hiding place in the livery stable before Kennedy sends his men out looking for us. As soon as we reach town, we'll get Doc Garrett to take a look at you.'

With Johnny by his side, Morgan walked to the fence where the four horses were tethered. They mounted two of the horses and Morgan led the other two as they set off for Dennison at a steady pace in the darkness.

With an aching head and an occasional

attack of dizziness, Johnny didn't enjoy the ride and he was glad when they finally reached town. They stopped outside the doctor's house and Morgan knocked on the door. It was a little while before Garrett, in his night clothes, and with a lighted lamp in his hand, answered the knock.

The doctor, surprised to see Morgan, exclaimed at the sight of the black eye and the rest of the wounds on Johnny's face. He quickly ushered them inside. As he examined Johnny's head, Morgan explained the situation to him and emphasised the need for himself and Johnny to go into hiding as quickly as possible. Then he left for the livery stable, leaving Johnny with the doctor.

When, after a short delay, Hal Jenkins answered Morgan's knock on the door of the house, Morgan quickly told him what had happened at the Crazy R.

'Johnny's at the doctor's place right now,' he said. 'Is that space in the loft ready for us to go into?'

117

'I cleared it out soon after you asked me about it,' replied Jenkins, 'and I laid a couple of mattresses on the floor in there, with some blankets.'

'Thanks,' said Morgan. 'I'm expecting that Kennedy and his men'll hit town round about daylight looking for us. I'll go back for Johnny now and we'll come to the stable as soon as the doc's finished with him.'

Morgan returned to the doctor's house, to find that he had treated the wounds on Johnny's face and was examining the bruise on the back of his head.

'He's going to have a sore head for a few days,' said Garrett, 'and maybe a dizzy spell now and again. But I don't reckon there's anything wrong with him that a little rest won't put right.'

'Thanks, Doc,' said Morgan. 'Hal Jenkins has the hiding-place ready for us in the stable loft. We'll go along to it now and stay there until it's safe to come out.'

The doctor handed Morgan some spare plasters and materials for bathing the wounds. Then, keeping in the shadow, the two men walked along the deserted street to the stable, where Jenkins was waiting. He looked with concern at Johnny's battered face.

'Everything's ready for you up above,' he said, 'and I've seen to the horses you brought back.'

'Thanks, Hal,' said Morgan. 'I reckon we might as well go in there now. Johnny here needs a rest after that beating he had. And I could do with a bit of sleep myself. Let's know when the Crazy R men have finished their search in town, will you?'

'Sure,' replied Jenkins.

They all climbed up to the loft and Morgan and Johnny went through the door into the space behind the false wall. An oil lamp was burning inside. Johnny lay down on one of the mattresses, Morgan on the other.

Jenkins closed the door and stood a number of planks against the wall so as to completely hide it. Then he climbed down from the loft and returned to his bed.

Eight

Kennedy and his foreman rode into town with six hands, all armed, just after daylight. Ignoring all protests, they made a thorough search of the town. The story Kennedy and his men put out was that a red-haired man called Trimble had been given a job as a ranch hand and had been caught stealing from the ranch-house safe during the night.

He had escaped, but had badly injured one of Kennedy's men in the process, and around $1,500 in banknotes had been stolen. No mention was made of an accomplice.

Kennedy himself, accompanied by Barlow, came to the livery stable. They thoroughly searched all the stalls and piles of fodder, then climbed up to the loft. Jenkins followed them.

Kennedy walked once around the floor of the loft, then stopped. Jenkins could see that he was looking closely at the loose planks standing up against the wall. Apprehensively, the liveryman stared at the rancher's back as he approached the planks and took hold of one.

He examined it closely, then stood it back against the wall. He turned to Jenkins.

'I need some timber exactly like this out at the ranch,' he said. 'Can you get some for me?'

'Sure,' said Jenkins, relieved. 'I can get it from Pueblo.'

'I'll get Hartley to give you the amount,' said Kennedy, then carried on, with Barlow, to search the liveryman's house.

Half an hour later, having drawn a blank, Kennedy and his men rode out of town. Shortly after they had left, Jenkins moved the planks in the loft and opened the door to the hiding place. He told Morgan and Johnny that the rancher and his men had all left.

'I expect they'll be searching the country around here,' said Morgan, 'and when they don't find us they might come back here for another look. We'd better stay up here for now and I'll watch out for them from the loft window there.'

Jenkins left and Morgan spoke to his friend. 'How're you feeling, Johnny?' he asked.

'Glad to be lying down,' said Johnny. 'My head's pretty clear now. I reckon I'll be all right in a day or so. You worked out a new plan yet?'

'One thing's clear,' said Morgan. 'Our chance of capturing Kennedy and Hartley at the ranch house has gone. They'll be on their guard now, not knowing why you were there and who it was that rescued you.

'Somehow, we've got to get the two of them away from the ranch on their own, so's we can grab them without interference from the Crazy R hands. I'm going to work on that problem right now.'

A little later, Jenkins brought up some

food and drink for them. Then Morgan sat for a while, his brow furrowed in thought, while Johnny rested. Later in the morning the doctor climbed up to have a look at Johnny's wounds.

'Everything's healing nicely,' he said. 'You got any plans for leaving town?'

'Not for a day or two,' replied Morgan.

'I'll look in tomorrow, then,' said Garrett.

Shortly after noon, when Jenkins brought a meal up for them, Morgan spoke to him about the banker Dawson. 'Does he have a house in town?' he asked.

'Yes,' replied Jenkins. 'He lives alone in a small single-storey house on the east side of town. He has a woman in each day to do the cleaning and fix him a meal at supper-time. She usually leaves the house around eight o'clock each evening.'

'So generally,' asked Morgan, 'he'd be alone in his house each evening after eight?'

'That's right,' replied Jenkins. 'Away from the bank, he's not really the sociable type.'

'Tomorrow evening, Johnny,' said Morgan, 'if you feel up to it, we'll pay the banker a visit.'

'I'll be ready,' said Johnny. 'All this hanging around ain't my style, as you know.'

Some of Kennedy's men, with Hartley in charge, rode into town the following day, to repeat the search for Johnny and his friend. Morgan saw them coming and once again the Crazy R men were forced to leave empty handed.

At nine o'clock that evening, Morgan and Johnny slipped out of the livery stable unobserved and moving along the backs of the buildings lining the street they reached the banker's house, which stood alone, near the edge of town.

Morgan looked around. No one was moving on the street. He walked up to the door and knocked. It was opened shortly after by Dawson. Morgan pushed his way in, followed by Johnny, who closed the door behind him.

The banker's face was a study as he recognized Morgan, whom he had assumed to be dead. Morgan ushered him through into the living-room before he spoke.

'A while ago, Dawson,' he said, 'just before Kennedy's man Hendrick was aiming to kill me, he told me that he had murdered my father and that Kennedy and his foreman had killed my mother. He told me as well, how you had helped Kennedy by preparing a fake bill of sale for my father's ranch.'

Dawson's face was ashen. His hand groped for the arm of a chair and he sank down on it. He looked a completely different man from the one Morgan has spoken to a while back about the sale of the Box C.

'I've been expecting that something like this might happen,' he said, 'and I'm relieved in a way. It's true that I forged that bill of sale. But when I did it, I thought that your mother's death was by accident or suicide. And I was forced into doing it by a hold that Kennedy has over me. It's a long story.'

'Let's have it,' said Morgan. 'We've plenty of time.'

Dawson told them how he'd been a banker in a small Missouri town. Ten years ago he had absconded with all the funds held in the bank and had moved to Dennison where, with plenty of capital to play with, and using a new name, he had opened the bank which he was now running as a very profitable business.

When Kennedy first arrived on the scene and visited the bank in Dennison, Dawson had been shocked to recognize him as a farmer with whom he had had dealings in Missouri. Kennedy had made no direct mention of Dawson's abscondment from Missouri, but he did make a veiled suggestion, with a hint of a threat in it, that the banker might be of some use to him in the future.

Then, on the day after Sarah Cassidy's death by drowning, Kennedy had called on Dawson early in the morning to tell him to forge a bill of sale for the Cassidy ranch. If he failed to do this, Kennedy said that he would see to it that Dawson was exposed as an embezzler.

'I did what he asked,' said Dawson. 'I copied a signature of your mother's that I have on my files. I didn't know then that he was a murderer as well as a thief.'

Morgan tended to believe Dawson's story. 'We'll have to hand you over to the law,' he said.

'I know that,' said Dawson.

'If you confess to the forgery in court and help us to get our hands on Kennedy and Hartley, there's a good chance the judge will take that into account,' said Morgan.

'I'll do what I can,' said Dawson. 'Maybe I'm a thief, but I don't hold with cold-blooded murder.'

'What we want to do,' said Morgan, 'is to get Kennedy and Hartley away from the Crazy R hands just long enough to capture them and take them to Denver without a lot of gunplay. The question is, how are we going to do that?'

The three men sat thinking for a while. Then the banker spoke. 'I think I could get the two of them to come to the bank,' he said, 'if I send a message out to the ranch tomorrow morning.'

'If you could do that,' said Morgan, 'it might solve the problem.'

'What I can do,' explained Dawson, 'is to tell Kennedy in the message that before the Box C ranch can finally be transferred to him, I have to send in to the authorities a statement signed by him and Hartley about the circumstances of the finding of the body. This isn't actually necessary, but Kennedy won't know that.

'I'll say that the matter's urgent. When do you want them to come into town?'

'Tell Kennedy you'll have the statement ready for them to sign at the bank at closing time at four o'clock,' said Morgan. 'Me and my partner'll be waiting in the bank to take them prisoner and all five of us should be on our way to Denver before dark.'

'You know, don't you,' said Dawson, 'that both Kennedy and Hartley'll be set on killing me when they find out what I've done?'

'We know,' said Morgan, 'and we'll see that it don't happen.'

'I'll spend tomorrow,' said Dawson, 'putting the bank's affairs in order. Nobody'll lose any money over my leaving this time.'

'Me and my partner'll be at the back door of the bank at three o'clock tomorrow afternoon,' said Morgan, 'just in case Kennedy and Hartley arrive early. Let us in and we'll figure out the best way to surprise them when they turn up.'

'I'll be expecting you,' said the banker.

On the way back to the stable Morgan and Johnny called in at the store, which was closed. Betty let them in through the rear door. Morgan told her about their plans for the following day.

'Don't you think,' she asked, 'that Kennedy might bring one or two of his men with him and Hartley?'

'It's possible,' said Morgan. 'If he does, me'n Johnny'll find some way of dealing with them.'

'It seems to me,' said Betty, 'that you

might need some help. Tomorrow morning I'm going to see Hal Jenkins and Doc Garrett. It's time some of us townsfolk took a stand against Kennedy. You two take care of Kennedy and his foreman. If they bring anybody else along, we'll attend to them.'

'Those are dangerous men you're talking about, Aunt Betty,' said Morgan.

'I know that,' she said, 'but you can't change my mind. It's something I've got to do. I'm pretty sure that Hal and the doctor will see it the same way.'

Back at the livery stable, Morgan told Jenkins about their conversation with Dawson and explained their plan for the following day. He asked the liveryman to have three saddled horses ready for himself, Johnny and Dawson by three o'clock the following afternoon. Kennedy and Hartley would be put on their own mounts.

After discussing a few more minor details, they all went to bed.

The following day, Morgan and Johnny stayed in the loft until just before three o'clock. Then, awaiting the right moment, they left the stable, slipped around to the rear door of the bank and knocked on it. Dawson let them in almost immediately and took them into his office.

It was a small room at the rear of the building, its door out of sight of the teller's counter at the front. Morgan looked around.

'If you bring them in this office when they get here,' he told Dawson, 'we'll wait for them behind the door. It should be easy enough for us to get the drop on them and take their guns.'

Leaving Johnny and Morgan in the office, Dawson went to work beside the teller at the counter. The teller left at four o'clock and a few minutes later Dawson saw Kennedy and Hartley approaching the door of the bank. He walked over to open it for them and hung up the CLOSED sign. As he was closing the door he saw two Crazy R hands on the boardwalk.

Kennedy seemed to be in a bad temper.

'You sure all this is necessary Dawson?' he asked. 'We're still hunting that man who robbed us three nights ago.'

'It *is* necessary if you want the Box C ranch,' Dawson replied. 'If you'll come to my office I have the papers ready for you to sign.'

Kennedy grunted and he and the foreman followed Dawson to the door of the manager's office. Dawson stood aside and ushered the two men in, then held back.

The two men were well inside the room before they realized it was already occupied by two grim-faced men holding levelled six-guns pointing in their direction. Kennedy and Hartley looked at Morgan in shocked surprise, realizing the futility of any opposition. They both raised their hands. As Johnny collected their revolvers Dawson came into the office.

'Damn you, Dawson,' said Kennedy. 'You set us up!'

'I was never happy working with murderers,' said Dawson, 'and I decided it was time for me to take my medicine.'

'You two,' said Morgan, 'along with Dawson here, are taking a ride with us to meet up with the US marshal in Denver. I'm sure he's going to be mighty interested when he hears what's been going on around here.'

'I saw two Crazy R hands out there,' Dawson told Morgan. 'They were on the boardwalk. I don't know where they were going.'

Morgan ordered Kennedy and his foreman to sit down with their backs to the wall. Then, leaving Johnny to guard them, he went to the front of the bank to look out of the window.

Watching from inside the livery stable, Jenkins and Garrett had seen the rancher and his foreman arrive. With some apprehension they saw that two Crazy R hands, Barlow and Ford, were with them. All four dismounted near the bank.

Kennedy and Hartley walked up to the door of the bank and disappeared inside.

The two hands hesitated for a moment. Jenkins was expecting that they would go into the saloon, but they both stepped on to the boardwalk, stood for a moment, then started walking towards the store.

Betty, watching through the store window, saw the two men approaching. Quickly, she ran behind the counter. Barlow and Ford came into the store and closed the door behind them. They walked up to the counter and stood facing Betty. Both men were scowling.

Before they could speak, Betty very carefully reached for the shelf under the counter. From it she took a double-barrelled American Arms 12-gauge shot-gun, cocked ready for firing, and lifted it into view, its barrels pointing midway between the bellies of the two men standing in front of her.

As Betty momentarily bent her head to check exactly where the triggers were, the raised hammers were plainly visible.

Both men froze, and Barlow's face turned

distinctly pale. The door of the store opened and Jenkins and Garrett came in, both carrying rifles. Quickly they disarmed the two men, then hastily moved well outside the blast pattern of the shotgun.

'Is that place in your loft ready for these two, Hal?' asked Betty.

Jenkins nodded.

'Let's get them over there, then,' she said.

Coming out from behind the counter, she told Barlow and Ford to walk slowly over to the livery stable.

The appearance of the small procession out on the street caused a minor sensation. It was led by the two worried-looking Crazy R men, hands raised, and treading very carefully.

Betty followed, carrying the cocked shotgun, with the prudent Garrett and Jenkins, both carrying rifles, walking slightly behind her. The few startled onlookers ahead of the procession moved with alacrity well out of its path. From the window of the bank, Morgan smiled as he watched the prisoners enter the livery stable.

Inside the stable, Jenkins climbed up the loft ladder, followed by the two prisoners. Garrett held the shotgun while Betty, with an agility belying her years, climbed up the ladder. Once in the loft, she took the weapon back from the doctor.

The prisoners were ordered into the space previously occupied by Morgan and Johnny. Before the door was closed behind Barlow and Ford, Betty spoke to them.

'For as long as we want to hold you in here,' she said, 'one of us three will be sitting out here holding this shotgun. If you make any noise or try to open the door, you can be sure it's going to be hit by a load of buckshot.'

She slammed the door to and pushed home the stout bolt which Jenkins had fitted earlier in the day. Then she handed the shotgun to Garrett, climbed down the ladder, and walked out into the street.

The attention of the onlookers standing outside the livery stable, was diverted to another spectacle when Kennedy and Hartley, hands bound, walked out of the bank with Morgan and Johnny close behind them. Dawson followed the others and closed the door behind him.

Betty walked over to Morgan. 'Ford and Barlow are prisoners up in the loft,' she said. 'We figure to keep them there all night.'

'Thanks,' said Morgan, 'and thank the other two for us. You sure made things a lot easier for us.'

Jenkins brought three saddled horses from the livery stable, and the five men mounted, rode out of town, and headed north. It was still daylight.

Barlow and Ford were released at ten o'clock the following morning by Jenkins and Garrett. The liveryman was holding the shotgun. Nobody had come into town during the night looking for the men from the Crazy R.

'By now,' said Jenkins, 'Cassidy and Trimble are well on their way to Denver. When they get there they're going to hand

Kennedy and Hartley over to the law for murder and robbery. If I were in the shoes of you and the other men at the Crazy R, I'd make myself scarce. You all must have had some idea of what was going on.'

'How about our guns?' asked Ford.

'Your guns stay here,' replied Jenkins, and, shortly after, the two men rode off towards the Crazy R.

Morgan and Johnny had an uneventful ride to Denver with the prisoners. They found US Marshal Turner in his office. He listened to their story, and that of Dawson, with considerable interest. Kennedy and Hartley declined his invitation to speak and he told a deputy to take them to a cell. Then he turned to Dawson.

'I can see,' he said, 'that you've helped to bring those two to justice. I'll make sure the judge knows about that. Meanwhile, I'll put you in a separate cell.'

He told Morgan and Johnny that he would check by telegraph with the US marshal at Fort Smith that they were who they claimed to be. He said that the judge would be holding court in Denver in five days' time and that they would both be required to give evidence.

At the subsequent trial, Hartley confessed to being present at the murder of Sarah Cassidy, and attempted to put the whole blame for her death on to Kennedy. He also told the court that he had heard Kennedy order Hendrick to kill Walt Cassidy, Morgan's father. In the event, both Kennedy and Hartley were sentenced to death by hanging. Dawson was committed to the state penitentiary for three years.

Morgan and Johnny called in to see the US marshal before leaving for Dennison.

'I guess you've still got some unfinished business to 'tend to,' said Turner.

'That's right,' said Morgan. 'So long as Hendrick's still running free.'

He asked Turner if he could arrange for the Crazy R cattle to be looked after until the ownership of the ranch was settled. The marshal said he would see that the matter was attended to.

When Johnny and Morgan arrived back at Dennison, Jenkins told them that the Crazy R hands had all left the day after Ford and Barlow had been released. And only that morning, he said, Jardine and Clark, Walt Cassidy's two hands, had ridden into town. They had heard of Kennedy's downfall and had come to see if Morgan could use them on the Box C.

Morgan told Jenkins that arrangements were being made for somebody to come and take charge of the Crazy R Ranch for the time being.

Morgan went to visit his aunt, then he located Jardine and Clark in town and asked them to move out to the Box C Ranch right away and start work. He put Jardine in charge, saying that he himself was leaving for a while. He told Jardine to take on another hand to help out. Then he and Johnny went to the store to have supper Betty Burke.

They were just finishing the meal when

there was a knock on the door. Betty answered it and came back with a telegraph message for Johnny. She and Morgan could see the concern on his face as he read it.

'It's from my mother in Julesberg,' said Johnny. 'My father's been took bad. A heart attack, she says. I've got to leave right now. I'm sorry Morgan. I was aiming to help you track Hendrick down.'

'You've done more than enough already Johnny,' said Morgan. 'I hope things ain't too bad when you get home. I'll get in touch when I come back.'

When Johnny had departed, Morgan went along to the telegraph office to send a message to the US marshal at Fort Smith telling him that his mother's killers had been dealt with by the law, and that he was setting out on the trail of Hendrick, the murderer of his father.

Nine

Morgan headed for Caldwell, a cattle town near the border between Kansas and Indian Territory. On his way there, near the end of his journey, he would pass close by the Gardner homestead, where he had lost his memory some time ago. He decided to call in to see them. He had thought constantly of Marion since he had last seen her.

Marion, working in the small garden close to the house, saw the approaching rider when he was some distance away. She could see that he was not a neighbour, but there was something familiar about him.

For a short while her view of him was obstructed by the barn. When he came in sight again, her heart skipped a beat as she realized that it was Morgan. She called to her parents inside the house, and ran to

142

meet him. Morgan dismounted as she reached him.

'I figured that maybe we'd never see you again,' she said.

'I'd never have left,' said Morgan, 'if I'd had any choice in the matter. I still haven't finished the job I set out to do. I think that my father's murderer is probably somewhere in this area.' Leading his horse, he walked by Marion's side up to the house, where Ben and Mary Gardner and their son Joey were waiting to greet him. They all went inside and Morgan told them what had happened since he left the homestead after recovering his memory. They listened to him with rapt attention.

Nearing the end of his story, he told them that he believed Hendrick might be somewhere in the area, and he hoped that he might come across somebody who had seen him around. He described Hendrick as bearded, stocky and mean-looking, with a distinctive scar running down the right side of his face.

Suddenly Joey piped up excitedly. 'I've seen him,' he said. 'In Barstow yesterday, when I went in on the buckboard with my pa. When he was in the store I was playing with Billy Cartwright around those old shacks back of the main street.

'I was chasing Billy when we nearly ran into this man. I think he'd just got off his horse. He was going into that shack where Mr Rogan lives. We both stopped, and I guess we stared at that mark on his face. He shouted at us and we ran back into the street. The next time we looked the horse was gone.'

'That mark on his face, Joey,' asked Morgan. 'Was it here?' He ran his forefinger down his right temple, past his eye, and down his cheek. 'And was the man about as tall as your father?'

'That's right,' said Joey, 'and he was mean looking, like you said.'

'Did you look at his horse, Joey?' asked Morgan.

'Yes,' said the boy. 'It was a big chestnut

with a white stripe down its face.'

'That sure sounds like Hendrick,' said Morgan. 'You keeping your eyes open like that has sure helped me a lot.'

He turned to Gardner. 'I'm going on to Barstow now,' he said, 'to see if I can find anybody who knows anything about the man Joey saw. And maybe I'll stay there in case he shows up again. D'you know anything about this man Rogan?'

'There's a feeling in town,' said Gardner, 'that maybe he's an ex-criminal. He don't do any work, but he seems to have plenty of money. I guess he's around sixty years old.'

'Maybe he's a friend of Hendrick's, then,' said Morgan. 'My best plan might be to keep an eye on that shack in case he turns up again. But first, I've got to see Marshal Binney in Caldwell. I'll ride over there tomorrow.'

The Gardners persuaded Morgan to eat supper with them and stay the night.

After breakfast the following morning, Morgan and Marion rode into Barstow, which lay a few miles east of the homestead, and on the way to Caldwell. When they reached town they had a look at Rogan's shack from the street. There was no horse outside. They parted, Marion to do some shopping, and Morgan to continue on to Caldwell.

When he reached his destination in the afternoon he sought out the marshal's office. He found Binney inside and introduced himself. The marshal was a rangy law officer with a reputation as an honest man and a tough enforcer of the law within the town limits of Caldwell.

'I got your message,' he told Morgan, 'and checked you out with the US marshal at Fort Smith. He reckons you're the best deputy he's got.

'I know that Hendrick and Kitchen are responsible for a lot of the crime around here, but the law's never been able to catch up with them. I know there's two other men in the gang. They're called Finney and Glover.'

'There hasn't been a bank robbery here since I sent that message?' asked Morgan.

'No,' replied Binney. 'We've been watching for any sign that one's due to happen, but none of the gang's been spotted in town yet.'

'I have news for you,' said Morgan. 'I'm pretty sure that Hendrick was seen in Barstow two days ago. He was visiting a man called Rogan, who's suspected of criminal activities in the past.

'I'm going back to Barstow first thing tomorrow and I'm going to keep a close watch on Rogan's shack. If Ty Hendrick turns up there again, I'll take him into custody and hand him over to the county sheriff. I'll be staying in the hotel in Barstow.'

'If there's any sign of the gang in Caldwell, I'll get word to you,' promised Binney.

After parting from Morgan, Marion spent some time shopping, then visited a friend. It was noon by the time she decided to ride

147

back to the homestead. But first, she thought, she would take another look at Rogan's shack. She mounted her horse and rode along the street towards a point from which the shack was visible.

She stopped abruptly as the shack came into view, and she saw that a big chestnut horse with a white stripe on its face was standing outside it. She backed her horse and dismounted, then looked across at the shack from the cover of a building. She had only been watching a few minutes when the door of the shack opened and a man came out, carrying a sack, and closed the door behind him. He tied the sack on the back of the chestnut.

The man was stocky and bearded, and although it was not possible to see a scar at that distance, Marion was sure that the man was Hendrick, and reasoned that he must be hiding out somewhere nearby. She decided that, in order to help Morgan, she would try to find out the location of the outlaw's hiding-place.

Hendrick mounted the chestnut and rode away from town in a southerly direction. Marion watched him from cover until he passed out of sight as he rode into a narrow gully some distance away. She mounted her horse and headed for the point where she had last seen him. When she got there, she was just in time to see him ride out of the far end of the gully and head towards a small hill further south, whose top was just visible. Then a dip in the ground hid him from view.

She rode up the gully and at the far end she stopped and had a careful look ahead. There was no sign of Hendrick, and she guessed he had passed behind the small hill which now she could clearly see ahead.

She carried on, but as she approached the hill she began to have misgivings and decided that if, when she reached it, there was no sign of Hendrick on the other side, she would return to Barstow.

Shortly after taking this decision she reached the foot of the hill and started to circle round it to see if she could spot the outlaw from the other side. Suddenly she was confronted by Hendrick as he stepped out from behind a large boulder standing at the base of the hill. As her horse reared, he grabbed the reins and told her to dismount. She could see the scar running down the right side of his face.

She obeyed, and he stood in front of her, scowling. Her heart sank.

'I'm curious to know why you're following me,' he said.

'I wasn't,' said Marion. 'I was just out for a ride. I'm Marion Gardner. I live near Barstow.'

'Lady,' said Hendrick, 'the kind of job I'm in, I'm an expert in knowing when I'm being followed, and I've been watching you for quite a while. Let's not beat about the bush. Once again, why were you following me?'

Apart from telling him the truth, which she couldn't do, Marion could think of no credible reply she could give to his question which might satisfy him.

'I was just out for a ride,' she said again.

Hendrick scowled at her. His concern was mounting. He was sure she had been following him and he had to find out why.

'You're a liar,' he said. 'I'm going to take you along to see some friends of mine. I'm pretty sure that between us we can get you to talk.'

Desperate, Marion turned and tried to run, but Hendrick, a powerful man, grabbed her and tied her wrists in front of her with a short piece of rope. Then he ordered her to mount her horse. He took the reins, mounted his own horse, and led the way south.

A few minutes later they crossed the border into Indian Territory, and seven miles further on they rode into a secluded ravine. A little way ahead Marion could see two stoutly-built shacks, one larger than the other. The smaller one of the two was located further up the ravine. Three men were standing outside the larger shack, one of them carrying a rifle. They stared at Marion as she and Hendrick approached.

The three were Herb Kitchen, Hendrick's brother-in-law, and Glover and Finney, members of the gang.

'Those three,' said Hendrick to Marion, 'are going to be just as keen as I am to find out just why you were following me.'

Kitchen, a short, thin-faced man, grinned and spoke to Hendrick as he stopped in front of them. 'What's this, Ty?' he asked. 'I didn't figure you for a ladies' man. Who's your friend? She sure is purty.'

Hendrick scowled. 'Says her name's Gardner,' he replied. 'What I want to find out is why she followed me right up to the border after I picked up those supplies from Rogan in Barstow – the ones I asked him to get for me a couple of days ago. She wouldn't say why she was trailing me. I didn't have no option but to bring her here. Maybe we can persuade her to talk.'

'That shouldn't be too hard,' grinned Glover.

'That's enough, Tom,' said Kitchen. 'Until we know exactly what this is all about, nobody touches the woman. I reckon the best way to find out is for one of us to ride into Barstow tomorrow morning. Everybody's bound to be talking about it if a woman's missing. Listening to the talk will maybe tell us why she was following Ty.'

'I reckon you're right, Herb,' said Hendrick. 'But who's going to go? Your face and mine are too well known from Wanted posters for either of us to show up in the centre of town. It'll have to be Zeb or Tom.'

'You go, Zeb,' said Kitchen to Finney. 'Go early tomorrow morning and find out everything you can about the woman. Meantime, we'll keep her fastened in the small shack. Check that bolt on the outside of the door. I noticed yesterday it had worked a bit loose.'

Marion, apprehensive about her future, was taken to the small shack and locked up inside. It contained little more than a bunk. A window, too small for her to pass through, was set in one of the walls. She lay down on the bunk, praying that Morgan, on his return from Caldwell, would find some way of rescuing her.

Finney rode into Barstow early the following morning, to find out that three small search parties had been formed to look for Marion, and were just about to leave town. He watched them depart, then went into the saloon, where he had a conversation with Hollister, the barkeep.

'This missing girl,' he asked. 'Does she live in town?'

'No,' replied Hollister. 'Her father Ben Gardner runs a homestead a few miles out.'

'And nobody has any idea where she might be?' asked Finney.

'That's right,' said the barkeep. 'She left a friend in town, saying she was going to ride straight out to the homestead, but she never arrived there.'

'Sounds like quite a mystery,' said Finney.

'It sure is,' said Hollister. 'And her folks are mighty upset over it. They're hoping that a friend of theirs, a deputy US marshal, might help them to find her. He's due back from Caldwell today.'

Finney pricked up his ears as the barkeep went on to tell him about Morgan's gun-battle at the homestead; his temporary loss of memory; and his intervention in the bank robbery in town.

'As soon as he got his memory back,' said Hollister, 'he hightailed it direct for Colorado. Something to do with his father being murdered there. Then he turned up here again two days ago. The talk is that he and the girl are pretty close.'

'What's the deputy's name?' asked Finney.

'It's Cassidy,' said the barkeep, 'Morgan Cassidy.'

Concerned, and somewhat puzzled by what he had just learnt, Finney rode back to Hendrick and the others. They came out of the cabin as he rode up and dismounted. He spoke to Hendrick.

'I remember you telling us,' he said, 'when you came back from Colorado, that you'd got rid of a deputy US marshal called Morgan Cassidy, who was the son of the rancher you shot from ambush.'

'That's right,' said Hendrick. 'What about it?'

'The odd thing is,' said Finney, 'that a deputy US marshal called Morgan Cassidy turned up in Barstow two days ago and it seems he's a friend of the missing girl and her family.'

He went on to pass on to Hendrick all he had heard from the barkeep.

'Damnation!' shouted Hendrick. 'I didn't see Cassidy's dead body down in that canyon, but I was sure that nobody could have taken that fall and lived. I just can't figure it out.'

'All the same, you reckon he's still alive?' asked Kitchen.

'From what Zeb says, he must be,' replied Hendrick. 'And I've got a strong feeling that he's on my trail. How he figured out I was in this area I don't know.'

He omitted to tell the others that he had

mentioned in Morgan's hearing, in Colorado, that he was due to join Kitchen to carry out a bank robbery in Caldwell.

'So long as he's around looking for you,' said Kitchen, 'we can forget about that bank job we're planning in Caldwell. I'm expecting to hear from the teller pretty soon that there's enough gold and cash in there to make a robbery well worth our while.'

'Yes,' said Hendrick, 'it's clear we've got to get rid of him pronto. He's the sort that never gives up. He's only got one idea in mind right now and that is to kill me or get me before a judge. Maybe we can use the girl to get hold of him.'

He turned to Finney. 'You say Cassidy's due back in Barstow today?' he asked.

'That's right,' replied Finney.

They all went inside the shack and spent some time discussing and agreeing a plan to eliminate Morgan.

Marion was still being held in the small shack, food and drink being brought to her when the outlaws had a meal. After the plan had been agreed on, Hendrick paid her a visit.

'There's a lot of folks looking for you,' he said, 'without any idea of where you might be. And I figure that Morgan Cassidy's one of them by now. We're aiming to fix it so that he'll be with you before long.'

Marion's heart sank, in the knowledge that Hendrick was now aware that Morgan was in the area looking for him. She wondered how the outlaws were planning to capture him. After Hendrick had left, she lay down on the bunk, sick with apprehension, staring up at the ceiling.

Ten

Morgan, on his return journey from Caldwell, was about three miles from Barstow when he saw a group of four riders approaching him. As they drew closer he was surprised to see that Marion's father was one of them. He stopped as the group reached him.

'I sure am glad to see you,' said Gardner. 'Marion's missing. She rode out of Barstow at noon yesterday and she ain't been seen since. We didn't start worrying till nightfall because sometimes she spends the afternoon with a friend in town. We've got three search parties out today, including this one.

'We've combed the area between Barstow and our homestead twice, and there ain't no sign of her. Now we're checking the rest of the area around Barstow.'

'I'm joining up with you,' said Morgan, greatly concerned at the news.

For the rest of the day the three parties continued a fruitless search for Marion until night had fallen. It was then called off until daylight.

After a restless night in his hotel room, Morgan rose early, ready to resume the search after a quick breakfast. Manson, the hotel owner, came up to him as he reached the foot of the stairs. He handed him an envelope addressed to Morgan and marked PRIVATE.

'This was pushed under the door some time during the night,' he said.

Morgan opened the envelope and took out a sheet of paper. Grim-faced, he closely studied the message printed in block capitals on the sheet. It read: WE'VE GOT THE GIRL. WILLING TO TRADE HER FOR YOU. COME ALONE TO FOOT OF HARLEY'S BLUFF TWO HOURS AFTER NOON. ANYBODY WITH YOU OR SEEN FOLLOWING

YOU AND SHE DIES. HENDRICK.

As Morgan finished studying the message, the hotel door opened and Gardner came in. Morgan handed the sheet of paper to him. He read it, then turned to Morgan, the strain showing on his face.

'Poor Marion,' he said. 'She must be worried sick. What do we do now?'

'Where is this Harley's Bluff?' asked Morgan.

'It's a well-known landmark around here,' replied Gardner. 'It's about ten miles south-east, not far from the border with Indian Territory.'

'In that case,' said Morgan, 'I'm sure that I saw it in the distance when I was riding back from Caldwell yesterday.'

'How can we get her back?' groaned Gardner.

'I know Hendrick,' said Morgan, 'and I know that he's quite capable of killing Marion if he doesn't get his way. First, we've got to stop the search. Then I've got to ride out to Harley's Bluff. And nobody must follow me. If anybody did, a look-out on the top of the bluff would spot him miles away.

'When I reach the bluff, I expect somebody'll take me to where they're holding Marion. From then on, I'll just have to hope that we get a chance to escape.' As he spoke, he knew what a forlorn hope that would be.

'Will they free Marion like they said, when they've taken you?' asked Gardner.

'Knowing Hendrick,' replied Morgan, 'I'm sure they won't. So don't expect her to come riding home today. It'll be up to ourselves to try and get away. I'll do the best I can for both of us.'

'I know you will,' said Gardner. 'I'm going to tell the others that we're stopping the search. And I'll ask them to stay in town or on their homesteads for the rest of the day.'

Morgan went to the general store, and after some discussion he came out with a couple of articles in his hands. They were items which the storekeeper said had not been around for a long time, but which had just come in that morning.

Morgan took the articles to Doc Bradley, with whom he spent half an hour before coming out and stuffing them in his saddle-bag.

He rode out of town alone, after telling Gardner not to lose hope. He reached Harley's Bluff just before two, and stood waiting at the foot of the north-facing cliff. Fifteen minutes later, two riders rounded the bluff from the south and approached him. They were Hendrick and Kitchen. Each was holding a gun in his hand.

The two outlaws dismounted, and Kitchen took Morgan's gun from its holster.

'I don't know, Cassidy,' said Hendrick, 'how you got away last time, but you can bet it ain't going to happen again. I'm going to see you dead this time. But first, we're going along to see your lady friend. We thought it would be nice to finish you off together.'

'I thought the deal was that you'd let her go,' said Morgan.

Hendrick grinned. 'You know as well as I do, Cassidy,' he said, 'that we can't do that.

She knows far too much. We don't want to lose that hide-out of ours. It's just right for us and we've been using it a long time.'

'Did you know that Kennedy and Hartley of the Crazy R in Colorado have both been hanged,' asked Morgan, 'and that Hartley testified in court that he heard Kennedy ordering you to kill my father?'

'No,' said Hendrick. 'The news ain't got here yet. Can't say I'm that interested. We'll be leaving soon. Don't want to keep your lady friend waiting, do we?

'You and the girl will maybe have to wait a day or two before we decide just how we're going to get rid of you. There ain't no rush. Nobody's going to look for you south of the border.'

They stayed a while to await the return of Kitchen, who had climbed the bluff to make sure there were no riders in sight. Then they headed south, and had soon crossed the border into Indian Territory.

When they reached the hide-out, Glover and Finney were waiting for them. Curious, they looked at Morgan.

'The girl's been no trouble?' asked Kitchen.

'None at all,' replied Finney. 'But I noticed her appetite ain't that good.'

'Put Cassidy in with her,' said Kitchen, 'and handcuff him, like the girl, with his hands behind him. We'll feed them for the time being.'

Morgan wondered how Kitchen came to be in possession of two pairs of handcuffs. It certainly didn't make the prospect of their escape any more likely.

Marion, lying on the bunk, sat up when the door of the shack opened and Morgan, handcuffed, was pushed inside by Finney.

'Company for you,' said the outlaw as he left, bolting the door behind him.

Marion jumped off the bunk and ran over to Morgan. She was close to tears.

'Have they hurt you, Marion?' he asked.

'No, I'm all right,' she replied, and told him how she had followed Hendrick from Barstow.

Morgan told her about the message from Hendrick which had resulted in his own capture.

'What happens to us now?' she asked. There was a note of despair in her voice.

'I'm hoping,' replied Morgan, 'that we'll get a chance to escape, but for the time being we'd better try and relax. I sure was worried when I got back from Caldwell and found you were missing.'

'It was silly of me to follow Hendrick,' she said. 'I realize that now. But I was thinking that maybe I could help you to find him.'

'I know that,' said Morgan.

They sat down on the bed and he asked her when meals were brought to the shack.

'Breakfast comes about eight,' she told him, 'then there's a meal about one in the afternoon, and supper at seven in the evening. Finney and Glover bring the meal together, and one of them takes the handcuffs off so's I can eat. One stays while I'm eating and the other comes back when I've finished, and handcuffs me again.'

Outside, Finney, who had unsaddled Morgan's horse, walked into the large shack to join the other three outlaws. He was carrying two large glass jars in his hands, each with a screw-on type top.

'Look what I found in Cassidy's saddle-bag,' he said. 'They're pretty scarce around here. Can't remember the last time I had any.'

Kitchen took one of the large jars in his hand and inspected it closely.

'Peaches in juice!' he said. 'They're a real favourite of mine.'

'Mine too,' said the other three in unison.

'I wonder what Cassidy's doing with them in his saddle-bag?' said Hendrick.

'I reckon he picked them up in Caldwell,' said Finney. 'I know he was riding back from Caldwell to Barstow yesterday. Maybe he was bringing them back for the Gardners.'

'Well,' said Kitchen, 'the Gardners lose out this time. I reckon there's enough peaches here for the four of us. They'll go down very nicely after bacon and beans at breakfast tomorrow.'

At supper time, Finney and Glover brought a meal for the prisoners, following the procedure which Marion had described earlier. When the meal was over and the handcuffs replaced, Finney told them that during the night he would be sleeping on a bedroll just outside the door of the shack.

He said that if there was any sign of them trying to get out he would shoot them down.

The two prisoners spent a restless night, Morgan lying on the floor of the shack. He could see no possible way in which they might escape during the night.

When morning came, Finney and Glover brought breakfast, and Glover took off the cuffs and left. Finney stood and watched them eat.

'We all took it mighty kind of you, Cassidy,' he grinned, 'to bring those peaches along for us. We've just had them at breakfast and pretty tasty they was too.'

'You're a greedy bunch,' said Morgan. 'I hope the whole four of you get the belly-ache.'

Finney grinned again. Shortly after, Glover returned and replaced the hand-cuffs. Then the two outlaws left.

When they had gone, Morgan explained to Marion the significance of the peaches, and time then passed slowly until the next meal was brought by Finney and Glover at half past one.

'Dunno why we're still feeding you two,' grumbled Finney. 'Seems like a waste of good food to me.'

Glover took the handcuffs off and departed. Then Finney stood inside the shack watching the prisoners eat. After a while he noticed that they seemed to be eating slowly and he grew impatient.

'Hurry it up!' he ordered. Then, suddenly, he belched loudly. He rubbed his stomach and belched again, even more loudly this time. Then, with no further warning, he doubled up as an agonizing combination of gastric and intestinal pain, worse than anything in his previous experience, grabbed him around the middle. Despite the intense discomfort, instinct drove him to reach for his gun.

Morgan was ready for action. He moved forward and, with his left hand, he grabbed Finney's gun hand before the outlaw could pull back the hammer. He beat the gun and the hand hard against the wall, and the gun dropped to the floor. Then, immediately, he landed a powerful right hand punch on the side of the outlaw's jaw which dropped him, unconscious, on the floor.

After picking up Finney's gun, Morgan bent down and gagged the outlaw with his bandanna, put a pair of handcuffs on him, tied his ankles together and dragged him to the middle of the floor of the shack. Then he lifted the heavy wooden bunk, turned it over, and dropped it on top of the outlaw's body. Finney groaned. He seemed to be coming round.

'That should keep him in here for a while,'

said Morgan, as he opened the door a little wider to look towards the other shack, a little way down the ravine. Nobody was in view, and he assumed that the other three outlaws were inside. He could see horses in the pasture beyond the shack, but figured it would be too risky to go there for mounts.

'Come on, Marion,' he said. 'As quickly as you can.'

As they left the shack he bolted the door behind them, then took Marion's hand and they ran up the ravine. Morgan's objective was for them to climb out of the ravine further up and head across the hard ground to the east, where he had noticed, when they rode in, an area studded with large boulders and rocky outcrops, and scarred with numerous small twisting gullies. Ideal country, in fact, for them to hide in.

As they ran, Morgan looked back down the ravine. There was still no sign of Hendrick and the others. He prayed for enough time to reach their objective. Seeing a place which would give them an easy climb out of the ravine, he turned and started to climb the slope, pulling Marion behind him.

Near the top, Morgan released Marion's hand as he climbed over the rim. She was standing on a piece of rock which was half embedded in the soil. But just as he stretched down to grasp her hand again, the rock came loose and she fell awkwardly twisting her ankle as she did so. She gave a cry of pain and slid down the slope for several yards before coming to a stop.

Hastily, Morgan climbed down after her. 'You all right Marion?' he asked.

Her face was white. 'My right ankle,' she said. 'I think I twisted it.'

Morgan glanced down the ravine. There was still no sign of Hendrick and the others. 'Try standing on it,' he said, lifting her up. But as soon as the slightest weight came on it, she cried out with pain.

'It's no good,' she said, looking at him in despair. 'I'm sorry. I can't walk on it.'

Desperately, Morgan looked down the ravine. There was no sign of the outlaws, but he couldn't risk carrying Marion to the cover he had been aiming for. It would take too long, and they could easily be caught out in the open. He looked around. A tall dense patch of brush growing at the bottom of the slope down into the ravine caught his eye. It was thirty yards further along the ravine from where he was standing.

He carried Marion back down the slope and along to the patch of brush. He pushed well inside it and laid her on the ground.

'I'll be back in a minute,' he said.

He retraced his previous path to the top of the slope, then made some marks which would indicate that he and Marion had left the ravine and had headed for the rough ground to the east.

He descended the slope at the same point as before. As he walked backwards towards the brush patch with a small branch covered with foliage in his hand, he did his best to remove any indication that he and Marion had gone into hiding there.

Just as he rejoined Marion and looked

down the ravine from their hiding-place, he saw the three outlaws spill out from the larger cabin one by one. All appeared to be bent forward, holding their stomachs, and moving around aimlessly.

Morgan lifted Marion up so that she could see the spectacle. As they watched, they saw one of the men, who looked like Hendrick, stagger over to the small cabin and go inside. Several minutes later, he reappeared with Finney, who staggered out holding his stomach and promptly fell to the ground. He picked himself up and made a stumbling run for the makeshift latrine set well away from the shacks.

Morgan laid Marion back on the ground. 'Try not to move that ankle, Marion,' he said. 'I'll take a look at it when I see what those four are going to do.'

As he watched, he saw Kitchen, then Hendrick and Glover, make a hurried dash for the latrine, and it was at least half an hour before they had all recovered sufficiently to start getting organized. Then

Glover brought three horses up to the cabin, where they were saddled.

Kitchen, Glover and Hendrick, rightly assuming that the escaping prisoners would go up the ravine, headed in that direction. Finney stayed behind.

Concealed in the brush, Morgan watched them as they approached. He told Marion to keep quiet. Shaken as they had been by a gut-wrenching ordeal which surpassed anything they had experienced before, the outlaws bore little or no resemblance to an efficient fighting machine. But they knew that it was vital to their own interests that the two fugitives be caught soon.

As the three riders drew closer, Morgan suspected, from their postures in the saddle, that they were still suffering a fair amount of internal discomfort.

When they reached the point from which Morgan and Marion had climbed up the slope, Hendrick dismounted and followed the tracks upwards. He disappeared over the top, and after a while he reappeared and climbed down to join the others.

'It's pretty clear,' he said, 'that they climbed out here and headed for cover. Can't see them, but they can't have got far. We'll have to ride after them and flush them out. And we'll have to move fast. There ain't much daylight left.'

They rode their horses down and out of the ravine, shouting to Finney as they passed, then swung round to start their search of the area for which Morgan had originally been aiming. Looking down towards the shacks, Morgan could see Finney moving around. He knelt down beside Marion.

'Three of the four have ridden off to look for us,' he said. 'They've left Finney on guard near the shacks. How's the ankle, Marion?'

'A bit easier when I don't move it,' she replied.

Gently he took off her boot. 'What I'm going to do now,' he told her, 'is bind your ankle and foot with something to stop the joint from moving. I reckon my shirt'll do.'

He took off his vest and shirt, then replaced the vest. He tore the shirt into strips about four inches wide, and one after the other, he wound the strips tightly around the foot, ankle and lower leg.

'That's easier,' said Marion. 'What do we do now?'

Morgan rose and looked down the ravine. 'Finney's still there,' he said, 'so we can't move out of here yet.'

He took Finney's gun from under his belt to check it. He examined it closely and swore under his breath. The hammer had been extensively damaged during his struggle with Finney and the weapon was useless.

'What we're going to do, Marion,' he said, 'is move out of here after dark. It's just struck me that the Chisholm Cattle Trail from South Texas to Caldwell runs not far east of here. I'm going to carry you till we hit the Trail.

'We're well into the trail-drive season and

there's a lot of cattle moving along the Chisholm, so I reckon there's a good chance of us meeting up with a trail-drive crew.'

'I can try walking,' said Marion.

'No,' he said, firmly. 'Do that, and you'd maybe ruin that ankle for good.'

They lapsed into silence for a while, then, despite the pain in her ankle and the precarious nature of their situation, Marion started giggling and it was a while before she could stop.

'What exactly was it that you put in with those peaches?' she asked.

Morgan grinned. He was pleased to see that the woman he intended to marry had such a well-developed sense of humour.

'I consulted Doc Bradley about it,' he replied, 'and he reckoned that the situation called for the strongest purgative he had. It was an Indian remedy he'd come across that was a lot more powerful than castor oil. The good thing about it was that it didn't have any special taste.

'We put enough in those two jars to give

each of those outlaws well over the normal dose. The doc said it would take anywhere between five and six hours to work, so it was pure luck that Finney was in our shack just at the right time.'

From time to time Morgan looked in the direction of the shacks. Occasionally Finney went inside the larger one, but most of the time he spent outside, sitting on a chair which he had brought out of the shack earlier.

It was half an hour after nightfall when Morgan heard, through the still night air, the faint sound of voices down the ravine, which shortly died away as the outlaws went inside the shack.

'I reckon they're back, Marion,' said Morgan. 'Time for us to leave.'

He picked her up in his arms and she put her arms around his neck. He walked out of the brush and down the ravine to the spot from which they had climbed out earlier. It was a difficult task, carrying Marion up the slope in the dark, but Morgan took it slowly, and eventually, breathing heavily, he stood at the top.

He took a quick look at the stars and started walking slowly due east, avoiding obstacles as he came to them. Occasionally there was a rise to climb, and uneven ground to stumble over, and as he progressed his stops for rest grew more and more frequent.

He asked Marion how she was feeling.

'I'm all right,' she said. *'I'm* not doing anything. It's you I'm worried about. How much longer can you go on like this?'

'I ain't done yet,' replied Morgan, as he bent down to pick her up again, a task he was finding more difficult each time.

He forced his legs into motion again and slowly trudged eastward. It was an hour and a half before dawn.

Eleven

On the Chisholm Trail, not far south of the border between Indian Territory and Kansas, it was half an hour before dawn. A stationary chuck wagon was surrounded by men, all but one lying asleep on the ground. A bedded herd lay nearby, with two night guards circling it in opposite directions.

The one active person near the chuck wagon was the cook, Theodore Blaney, Theo to his close friends. He was preparing a breakfast of bacon, beans and biscuits for the crew. He was a small active man in his sixties, bald, and sporting a luxuriant white beard.

When all was ready he started to bellow his daily invitation to the men to come to breakfast. But he barely got one word out before his attention was caught by a man weaving and staggering towards him with a woman in his arms.

The cook ran to one of the sleeping men and shook him by the shoulder. 'Mr Leary!' he called. Then he ran up to Morgan and helped him to lay Marion on the ground.

Leary, the trail boss, sat up and looked across at the two strangers. Hastily, he pulled on his pants and boots and donned his shirt, then he walked quickly over to Marion and the two men standing over her. The other trail hands, who had been lying on the ground, quickly dressed and followed him.

'This is Mr Leary, the trail boss,' said the cook to Morgan.

'My name's Cassidy,' said Morgan. 'I'm a deputy US marshal. And this is Miss Gardner. Her father runs a homestead over the border. But before I tell you how we come to be here, maybe we could make Miss Gardner's ankle a bit more comfortable. I reckon it's badly sprained.'

'As well as being the cook,' said the trail boss, 'Mr Blaney here is the medical expert in this outfit. Take a look at it, Theo.'

The cook unwound the makeshift bandage and closely examined the ankle.

'A bad sprain is what it is,' he said. 'It's not broken. I'm going to bandage it up tight, then I'll clear a space in the chuck wagon where the lady can lie comfortable. She ain't going to walk on that leg for a while. She needs to keep that ankle still.'

While the cook was attending to Marion, Morgan described to Leary and the others the events which had led to their appearance at the camp. His account of how he and Marion had managed to escape from the outlaws gave rise to considerable hilarity on the part of his audience. Most of them, from time to time, had found it necessary to have recourse to the large bottle of castor oil in the cook's medicine box.

'First of all,' Morgan went on, 'I'm going to get Miss Gardner home to her family. Then I'll go looking for Hendrick and the others.'

Shortly after this, Marion was lifted into

the chuck wagon and the cattle were put on the trail. Towards the end of the day's drive, Morgan rode up to the trail boss, riding at the head of the column. He said he had decided to build a travois for Marion. Then, if Leary would loan him a couple of horses, he would set off in a north westerly direction for Barstow, at first light the following morning.

'That's a good idea,' said Leary. 'If you use two long poles, with a bit of spring to them, it'll be a lot more comfortable for the lady than riding in the chuck wagon. And she'll get home a lot quicker.

'There's some trees standing near our bed-ground for tonight. I'll get one of the hands to help you with the travois when we get there. As for the horses, you're welcome to them. I'll get the wrangler to pick out two from the remuda. And I sure hope you catch up with the men you're after.'

'Thanks,' said Morgan. 'I'll see the horses get back to you at Caldwell.'

They built the travois that evening and

Marion and Morgan were ready to leave at daylight. A comfortable platform had been provided for Marion to lie on and her sprained ankle had been secured so as to keep any movement to a minimum. The trail hands assembled to see them off.

Marion thanked the cook for his care.

'Shucks, miss,' he replied, 'it weren't nothing. And it pleasured me to see you here. When you think that for the last three months the only company I've had is cattle and horses and this ugly-looking bunch of rowdy trail hands you see here, you'll understand it was like a breath of fresh air when I saw a pretty lady like yourself turn up in camp.'

Grinning, the hands gave a wave as the two left, Morgan riding ahead and leading the horse which was pulling the travois. They moved as fast as they could, without causing undue discomfort to Marion, and arrived in Barstow in mid afternoon.

Their arrival caused considerable excitement in town and a small crowd collected and followed them to Doc Bradley's house. Morgan spoke to the people standing watching them.

'Would somebody ride out to the Gardner homestead,' he asked, 'and tell them that Marion's in town at the doctor's house? Say it's a sprained ankle, nothing else.'

A young man at the back of the crowd replied. 'I'll do it,' he said, and ran to a horse at a hitching rail. A moment later he was racing out of town.

Doc Bradley gave Marion's ankle a thorough examination.

'The cook was right,' he said. 'A few weeks' rest, and this'll be fine. I'll take Marion out to the homestead in my buggy. It's pretty well sprung. We'll probably meet her folks on the way.'

And so it was. Half-way there, with Morgan riding alongside the buggy, they met the buckboard carrying Gardner and his wife and son. After a joyful reunion they all headed for the homestead.

Later in the evening, when Marion was

settled in, Morgan told her that he was going to renew his search for Hendrick.

'I'm sure,' he said, 'that by now he and the others will have given up the idea of robbing the bank at Caldwell. They'll know that the law is searching for them. They'll be looking for a new hiding-place. And the best place to look for that is in Indian Territory. They'll probably move further south.

'First, I'm going to the ravine where they were hiding out. Then I'll sweep the country south, to see if I can find anybody who's seen them. If I do manage to locate them I'll ask Fort Smith for help.'

'You'll come back here when the job's done?' she asked.

'Just as soon as I can,' he replied. 'Then we'll talk about you and me and the future.'

The next morning, Morgan sent messages to Fort Smith and Marshal Binney in Caldwell, advising them that Hendrick and the others had left their hide-out in Indian Territory, and that he was now searching for them.

He rode straight to the hide-out. He saw what he thought were faint tracks of the outlaws heading south but lost them after a mile or so. He continued riding south, searching for tracks without success, and late in the afternoon he rode into the small town of Lantry.

Here, he had a stroke of luck. The storekeeper recognized Hendrick, from Morgan's description, as a man who had been in the store several days ago. When Hendrick had left the store, he had paused on the boardwalk to talk to three other men standing there.

Curious about the four men, the storekeeper had moved up to the open window, and through it he had heard snatches of the conversation. He had heard one of the men ask Hendrick how far it was to Morello, and just after this a name 'Fuller' was mentioned. Then the four men had moved away.

'In case you don't know it,' said the storekeeper, 'Morello's about thirty miles south of here.'

Morgan went to the telegraph office and sent a message explaining the situation to the US marshal at Fort Smith, and asking that a couple of deputies be sent to join him at Morello. Then he went to take a room at the small hotel.

He arrived at Morello the following afternoon. It was little more than a single dusty street, with the usual store, hotel, livery stable, saloon, and a few other buildings and shacks. He took a room at the hotel, then handed his horse in at the livery stable. Without his lawman's badge, which he had lost in Indian Territory before his first visit to the Gardner homestead, his status as a deputy US marshal was not evident to the people in town.

On his way in he had noticed, and had waved to, a bearded elderly man sitting on an armchair on the porch of a small shack near the edge of town. He walked back along the street and stopped near the shack.

The man in the armchair observed Morgan with a keen eye. A veteran Indian fighter, now almost crippled with an old leg wound caused by a Sioux arrow, Hec Ryder had decided, some time ago, to spend his declining years in Morello. A familiar figure, seated on his porch, there was little he didn't know about the affairs of his fellow townspeople.

'I'd appreciate a few words with you,' said Morgan. 'My name's Cassidy.'

'Hec Ryder,' said the veteran. 'Step up and take that chair.' He took another keen look at Morgan, starting with his face, then moving down to his six-gun, then his boots.

'Let me guess,' he said. 'I'd be surprised if I ain't looking at a lawman.'

Rather taken aback, Morgan could see no point in denying it. 'It shows?' he asked.

'It shows,' said Ryder. 'Something in the eye, I reckon. What did you want to talk about?'

'Does the name "Fuller" mean anything to you?' asked Morgan.

'It sure does,' replied Ryder. 'That's the name of a man who built a big house ten miles south-east of here, plumb on top of a hill in the middle of an area of level ground. You want to know a bit more about him and the place he built?'

'As much as you can tell me,' replied Morgan.

Ryder settled back in his chair and told Morgan how, three years ago, an Englishman called Fuller had arrived in the area, complete with a building crew, lumber, and all other necessary building materials for the job they had come to do.

First, they built a road up the hillside. Then they hauled all the building materials up to the flat area on the top of the hill and built a big house and stable and a few other buildings. When it was finished, the building crew all left.

'Did anybody from Morello do any work there?' asked Morgan.

'No, they didn't,' Hec Ryder replied. 'In fact, nobody from round here has actually been to the house. The storekeeper rode out one day to see if he could do any business with Fuller, but he didn't get any further than an armed guard stationed three-quarters of the way up the road to the top.

'The storekeeper said there was a big sign there saying that trespassers would be shot. The guard told him that all the supplies needed were freighted from somewhere down south.

'And what's more,' Ryder concluded, 'never once have we seen anybody from Fuller's place in town.'

'Did it ever come out,' asked Morgan, 'just why this Fuller built the house up there?'

'Soon after the buildings were finished,' said Ryder, 'there was a rumour that Fuller was a rich man, a little on the crazy side, who liked his privacy, and who had brought a big telescope with him for taking a look at the moon and the stars and suchlike.'

'So nobody in town,' asked Morgan, 'has ever seen Fuller or any of the people he has up there with him?'

'That's right,' said Ryder.

Morgan decided that he could trust the veteran.

'The reason I'm interested in Fuller's place,' he said, 'is because I reckon that maybe it's being used as a hiding-place by outlaws running from the law.

'Fuller would have to lay out a lot of money to build the place, but think of the returns he'd be able to get from outlaws flush with the proceeds of robberies. Indian Territory is a favourite hiding-place for criminals of all kinds, and I reckon that once the word got around, it wouldn't be long before Fuller's place was pretty near full most of the time.'

'If you're right,' said Ryder, 'it explains quite a lot. What're you going to do about it?'

'I've asked Fort Smith for more deputies,' replied Morgan, 'and while I'm waiting for them I'm going to ride out there and look at the place from a distance. When the deputies get here, we'll take a proper look at the buildings on top of the hill. I'd be obliged if you'd keep all this to yourself for the time being.'

'Right,' said Ryder. 'If anybody asks, I'll say you just called by to have a chat about the weather. Let me know how things are going, won't you? It's usually pretty dull around here, but I can see that maybe things are going to liven up considerably.'

'I'll keep in touch,' Morgan promised.

The following morning, Morgan headed for Fuller's place, taking his field-glasses with him. He stopped on the edge of the plain, behind two large boulders about half a mile distant from the base of the hill on which the buildings had been erected. There was a small gap between the boulders at eye level and through this he scrutinized the hill and the buildings on top of it.

He could clearly see the road, which took a winding course up the hill to maintain a reasonable gradient. Three quarters of the way up, he could see two men standing by the side of the road, with two horses close by.

At the top of the hill the road disappeared among the buildings. The largest building was considerably bigger than the average ranch house. On top of it was a structure which, to Morgan, had all the appearance of a watch tower.

Morgan left his cover and returned to Morello. He was pretty convinced by now that Fuller was harbouring criminals. He decided that nothing further could be done until help arrived.

Twelve

Two days later, two deputy US marshals, Bernie Whitmore and Jon Winter, rode into Morello around one in the afternoon, and located Morgan in the hotel, where he was just starting a meal. They sat down and ordered for themselves.

Morgan had met Winter a couple of times in Fort Smith, but Whitmore was a stranger to him. Winter handed Morgan a deputy US marshal's badge to replace the one he had lost a while ago.

'The marshal's put you in charge of this operation, Morgan,' he said. 'He'd have liked to send more deputies, but we're all he can spare just now. How about putting us in the picture?'

Morgan passed on all the information he had got from Ryder and from his own recent inspection of Fuller's place through field-glasses.

'Tomorrow morning,' he said, 'we'll all ride out there. You and me, Jon, we'll ride up the hill to see Fuller. Bernie will stay out of sight. If we don't get back to him before dark, he won't go up the hill himself, but he'll get in touch with Fort Smith pronto.'

'This might turn out to be something big?' Winter suggested.

'Maybe,' replied Morgan. 'Just think of it. It's a big place. Could be quite a few criminals in there. And they'd be the ones operating in a big way, with plenty of money coming in. Just the ones we want to get our hands on, in fact.'

They set off early the following morning. On the way out of town Morgan introduced his partners to Hec Ryder and gave the veteran a rough idea of their plans.

They left Whitmore behind just before they rode on to the plain surrounding Fuller's place. Morgan and Winter headed for the point where the road started to climb the hill. On reaching it, they rode slowly up the slope towards the two guards, both standing looking towards them, with rifles in their hands.

Both guards were surly-looking characters, wearing sidearms. One was tall and thin; the other was of medium height, and stocky. They stepped out into the road as the deputies drew close. Morgan and Winter stopped in front of them.

'This is as far as you go,' said the thin man, curtly. 'This is private property.'

'We're Federal officers,' said Morgan. 'We're here to see the owner of this place on official business.'

'I've got my orders,' said the guard. 'Mr Fuller don't want to see nobody that he ain't invited himself.'

'One of you had better tell Fuller,' said Morgan, 'that two Federal officers want to see him, and if you don't let them through there'll be a lot more deputies coming from Fort Smith, or maybe a troop of cavalry, to find out just why he's so cagey about letting anybody on to his place.'

The two guards withdrew out of earshot of the deputies, and after a short consultation the stocky one mounted his horse, rode up to the top of the hill, and disappeared from view.

He was gone for over half an hour, during which the other guard maintained a surly silence. When he reappeared in view, he rode slowly down to the deputies and asked them to follow him up to the house. As they reached it, a door opened and a man stood in the doorway.

He was a big man, fair-haired and heavy-jowled, wearing a neatly-trimmed goatee beard. He was impeccably dressed in Eastern-style clothing and his welcoming smile displayed a perfect set of teeth.

'Gentlemen,' he said, affably. 'I must apologise for the bad manners of my staff. My orders to turn callers away were not intended to apply to officers of the law like yourselves. Please come inside.'

He led them into a big room, furnished

with a large number of comfortable arm-chairs and small tables. One wall was fully lined with bookcases containing a good selection of books. There was a big fireplace at one end of the room. They all sat down.

'Now, gentleman,' said Fuller. 'What can I do for you?'

'We're deputy US marshals,' said Morgan. 'Our job is to try and keep Indian Territory free of all the criminals that come here because they think it's a good place to hide out from the law.'

'And a very praiseworthy job it is that you're doing,' said Fuller.

'So,' said Morgan, 'when we happen to ride by and see this big house stuck on top of a hill in the middle of nowhere, we're naturally curious about it.'

'Naturally,' said Fuller. 'Being curious must be an essential part of your job. What do you want to know?'

'Well,' said Morgan, 'what we were curious about was why you built a big place like this on the top of a hill. Apart from anything else, the cost must have been pretty high.'

'As it happens,' said Fuller, 'I'm a rich man, so the cost wasn't a matter that concerned me. As for me building it on top of a hill, my noble forebears in England in mediaeval times felt more comfortable living in a castle built on high ground. It gave them an advantage when they were being attacked by their enemies.

'I must have inherited this instinct to live in a place from which I can look down and see all that is going on around me. When I was travelling through this area a few years ago, looking for a place to settle, I saw this hill and decided that right on top of it was where I wanted to live.'

Smiling, he offered to show them around the place. Morgan accepted the offer.

'I'm very proud of this establishment,' said Fuller. 'I want you to see everything I've done here. This room is our lounge and library, of course.' He led them into the room next door. 'And this is our dining-room.'

Morgan saw that the room had two doors, one from the outside and one from the lounge. There were also two swing doors which, he thought, probably led into a kitchen. He looked at the large, handsome dining-table and the comfortable chairs, and saw that it would seat at least twenty people.

'I expect you're wondering,' said Fuller, 'why everything is on such a large scale here. The fact is, that although I'm alone just at the moment, I have quite a number of friends and acquaintances visiting me from time to time.

'As a matter of fact, I'm expecting a Congressman here, with some of his friends, in a couple of weeks' time.'

Morgan looked suitably impressed. 'You'll have quite a few employees, then?' Morgan said.

'Yes,' replied Fuller. 'I have Mexican men and women to look after the needs of myself and the guests and guards. I have ten guards altogether working in shifts. As you pointed out earlier, criminals abound in the Territory, and I must protect my influential guests. I have guards posted on the road, day and night.'

He took them over to the large stable, which was, Morgan noticed, equipped with a small blacksmith's-shop.

'As you see,' said Fuller, 'we have plenty of horses to cater for guests who might fancy taking a ride down below.'

He led them back to the house, then up to the bedroom area. A Mexican servant, a woman, came out of the first bedroom they came to. Fuller took them inside the room to look around. Morgan commented on the quality of the furnishings.

'I have to keep a reasonable standard,' said Fuller. 'As I said, I have some quite influential people coming here to stay with me.'

They followed him along a corridor on to which the bedrooms, twenty in all, opened. The doors were open, and the two deputies could see that all the rooms were empty.

'I think you'll be interested in my next

exhibit,' Fuller said, as he led the way up some steps to the flat roof of the building and walked to the foot of the tower which Morgan had seen from below. He climbed the ladder attached to the side of the tower and entered a small room at the top. Morgan and his partner followed him.

Inside the room was a large brass telescope, so mounted that it could be rotated through 360° and could be lifted through the roof when this was slid aside. Morgan noticed that it could be used to detect anyone approaching the hill from any direction.

Fuller pointed to the telescope. 'A hobby of mine, gentlemen,' he said, 'and another reason for me living up here, where the air is clearer. Through this instrument I study the wonders of the universe.'

'Apart from being able to use the Big Dipper and the North Star to find out where north is, it's all a big mystery to me,' said Morgan.

Fuller took them down below and showed them the kitchen and the servants' accommodation, also the small building which provided accommodation for the guards. Eight of the guards were inside, relaxing.

'And that's about all, gentlemen,' said Fuller, as he led them to the top of the road leading down the hill. 'I hope I've managed to satisfy your curiosity.'

'You sure have,' Morgan replied. 'I'm sorry we troubled you. But it was mighty interesting to see what you've done up here. We'll carry on now with the job we were doing when we spotted this place. We've twenty miles to ride before nightfall.'

As Fuller watched the two deputies ride off, the expansive smile with which he had bidden them farewell gradually faded away.

Morgan and his partner passed the two guards without speaking to them and they themselves remained silent until they rejoined Whitmore. They told him what had happened, then rode off in the direction of Morello.

'D'you reckon that Fuller's telling the truth?' asked Whitmore.

'I'm sure he isn't,' Morgan replied. 'He might think he's fooled us, but his story just don't ring true.'

'I agree with Morgan,' said Winter.

'I think,' said Morgan, 'that there are criminals staying up there right now. From the time they spotted us through the telescope riding on to the plain, to the time we met Fuller at the house, it would be possible for them to hide the guests away somewhere and remove any evidence that anybody was staying there. I'm sure Fuller has his people well enough organized to see to that.'

'What's our next move then?' asked Winter.

'We'll stop right here,' said Morgan. 'Then, after nightfall, I'm going to try to get up to the top of the hill without them seeing me. We've got to have evidence that Fuller's harbouring criminals. Maybe I can get that evidence. If I do, we'll decide on our next move when I get back. Maybe we'll have to send for reinforcements.'

'But how can you get up without being spotted?' asked Whitmore.

'I noticed when we were riding up and down the hill,' said Morgan, 'that there seemed to be one possible way, apart from using the road, of climbing to the top on foot without alerting the guards. So I'm going to give it a try that way.

'When we get back there after nightfall, you two can wait for me with my horse, down on the plain. If I'm not back with you before dawn, get in touch with Fort Smith. I don't reckon it would be safe for you to go in there alone looking for me.'

Reaching the plain after nightfall, they rode up to a position at the foot of the hill well away from the road. The night was dark.

Morgan started his climb, trying to follow the route he had picked out while riding up and down the hill earlier in the day. He had wound a lariat around his middle, in case it was needed.

The first forty yards or so were easy going,

but after that the gradient increased considerably. He lay flat on the slope, face down, and crawled upwards, helping himself on by grabbing and pulling on the sparse vegetation as he progressed.

Then he came to a section where the surface was composed of smooth rock with a thin coating of soil. He edged his way up this with difficulty, but after progressing seven yards or so he lost control and slid back the same distance.

Moving sideways towards the road, he found a more suitable surface to climb and continued his upward progress. Resting for a moment, he heard the two guards talking to one another abreast of him, not far away.

He moved on, as silently as he could, until he reached a point about twelve feet below the flat top of the hill. Here, the slope gave way to a sheer wall of rock which was impossible to climb.

Looking upwards, he could see, silhouetted against the night sky, a rock projecting from the ground at the top of this sheer wall. He unwound the lariat from his middle and made an overhand upward toss for the rock. Twice he missed, but at the third attempt the loop dropped over the rock.

Minutes later, he was crouching at the top of the sheer wall, breathing heavily, and looking across at the buildings. He could see no sign of guards and guessed that Fuller relied entirely on the ones stationed on the road.

The windows of the dining-room were visible to him, about fifteen yards away. The lights were on inside and the curtains were not drawn. He ran over to the wall adjacent to one of the windows and peered inside.

The big dining-table was almost fully occupied and Mexican men and women were moving around serving a meal. Morgan ran his eyes around the eighteen men seated at the table. Fuller himself was seated at the head of the table, playing the genial host to perfection. Next to him Morgan saw Kitchen, Hendrick, Finney and Glover.

Then he whistled under his breath as he recognized, in turn, moving from one window to another, the notorious outlaw gang leaders Donovan, Atkins, Bolton and Skipton, together with members of their gangs. These men were all guilty of widespread murder and robbery involving large sums of money, and had so far evaded capture.

Looking carefully at the men seated nearest to him, Morgan could see that they were not wearing sidearms. He moved along to the wall of the lounge and looked in through one of the windows. The room was empty except for a Mexican woman who was wiping the table tops.

He ran over to the building housing the guards and looked inside. Eight men, including the two who had stopped them on the road earlier in the day, were taking a meal inside. Two Mexican women were serving them.

Morgan reckoned that he had seen enough, and that his chances of remaining unobserved were rapidly dwindling. He returned to the point where he had earlier arrived at the top of the hill and climbed down the rope to the foot of the sheer section of the wall.

He shook the loop of his lariat free of the rock above, and carefully retraced his path to the bottom of the slope. When he rejoined his two partners, both men were very relieved to see him. He told them what he had seen above.

'This is the chance of a lifetime,' he said. 'A chance to capture five of the most wanted outlaw gangs west of the Missouri, all in one go. Let's get away from here, then we can talk about it. One thing's certain. With all those guards and outlaws up there, we can't risk going up with only three men. I'll have to ask for more deputies.'

They headed east for the town of Wanoka, the nearest one with a telegraph office. Arriving there two and a half hours later, they took rooms at the hotel, then spent the next hour working on a plan for the capture of Fuller and his criminal guests.

They slept for a few hours, and after breakfast Morgan went along to the telegraph office. He sent a long message to the US marshal at Fort Smith advising him of the opportunity of their making an important capture, and of the need for secrecy. The message said that a further seven deputies would be needed to ensure success and that the men should join Morgan at Wanoka. Handcuffs would be needed for twenty-eight prisoners.

Morgan impressed on the telegraph operator the need for secrecy, then went back to the hotel to wait for the reply. He could imagine the flurry of activity his message would cause at Fort Smith.

He knew that the marshal there had a force of around 200 deputies at his disposal, and he was certain that in view of the potential gains which could result from the operation, he would send the seven that Morgan had asked for. But he would have to send messages withdrawing them from other operations and ordering them to join Morgan.

Four hours or so later the telegraph operator brought the reply from Fort Smith. It read: SEVEN DEPUTIES WILL ARRIVE WANOKA IN 5/6 DAYS. YOU WILL TAKE CHARGE OF OPERATION.

Morgan showed his partners the message. 'All we can do now is sit and wait,' he said, 'and hope that none of those outlaws leaves Fuller's place before we get there.'

Five deputies rode in five days later and the other two arrived during the morning of the following day. None of them had been told of the exact nature or location of the operation.

Morgan quickly acquainted them with the facts and discussed with them his plan for capturing Fuller and the outlaws.

They left in the afternoon, timing their departure so that they would arrive on the plain below Fuller's place just after night-fall. It was vital, as Morgan had explained to the deputies, that they arrive at the top of the hill just as the evening meal was being served.

They left their horses at the bottom of the hill, and with Morgan in the lead, the ten deputies climbed the slope, following the route which Morgan had taken a week previously. They carried handcuffs with them. When they came to the sheer wall at the top, Morgan threw the loop of his lariat over the rock as before, and one by one they climbed up the rope and stood on the flat surface above.

Two of the deputies left to go down the road to capture the two guards, who would be unlikely to be anticipating danger from above.

Morgan took three deputies with him to the outside of the dining-room wall and Winter took three to the outside of the building where Morgan had seen the guards eating a week before.

Morgan looked through a window of the dining-room. The meal was being served and he was relieved to see that all the outlaws he had seen on his last visit were present. Fuller, as before, sat at the head of the table, beaming on the assembly.

Winter, looking through a window of the other building, saw that the guards, eight in all, were busy eating. He ran back to Morgan. 'They're in there,' he said.

'We'll both go in now, then,' said Morgan, and Winter returned to the other building.

Morgan pushed open the door of the dining-room and ran in, followed by three deputies. All were holding six-guns. They stationed themselves two on each side of the table, behind the seated outlaws. Two women servants screamed and ran into a corner.

'Stay still!' shouted Morgan. 'There are four guns on you. We're deputy US marshals. You're all under arrest. Anybody moves, and they're going to get shot.'

Nobody moved.

Fuller, recognizing Morgan, started to say something, then changed his mind. Hendrick, who was sitting on the opposite side of the table from where Morgan was standing, also recognized him.

'Damn you, Cassidy!' he said, and rage boiled up inside him. He reached for the .41 Derringer in the pocket of his vest, but before he could swing the pistol up and round to bear on Morgan, the deputy shot him in the upper part of his right arm and the Derringer dropped to the floor. Hendrick yelled out in pain and slumped back in his chair.

Quickly, Fuller and the outlaws were all handcuffed with their hands behind them, still seated at the table. Then they were searched for hidden weapons.

At the same time that Morgan entered the dining-room, Winter, followed by three deputies, burst into the room where the guards were eating, and shouted to them to stay still. Only one man disobeyed and reached for his gun. The deputy behind him rapped him over the head with the barrel of his pistol and the guard, stunned, slumped down in his chair. Then all eight men were handcuffed and their arms were taken.

The servants put up no resistance and were herded into the lounge for the time being. Shortly after this, the two guards from the road below were brought in by the two deputies who had been sent to capture them. They were handcuffed and placed with the others.

Morgan decided to hold the prisoners in the house, with the servants providing the necessary meals, until jail wagons could be provided to transport them all to Fort Smith. He sent a deputy to Wanoka with a message to be telegraphed to the US marshal, advising the successful outcome of the operation and asking for jail wagons to be sent as quickly as possible.

A search of the bedrooms and the prisoners' clothing yielded a rich haul of cash, gold dust and other valuables.

One puzzle remained to be solved. Where had the outlaws been hiding when Fuller showed Morgan and his partner round the establishment? Morgan went to see the Mexican in charge of the servants and asked him about the hiding place. It didn't take him long to convince the man that he'd be wise to cooperate.

The Mexican led him to a corner of the lounge and lifted the carpet to reveal a trapdoor. Morgan lifted this, and carrying a lighted lamp he descended a flight of steps. At the bottom he found himself at the beginning of a shored-up tunnel which had been dug under the house. There was plenty of room in it for Fuller's full complement of guests. He returned to the lounge.

He could visualize the scene when he and Winter had first ridden on to the plain below the hill, to be spotted by the look-out in the tower. The initial alert would have been sounded. Then, when Morgan had insisted on seeing Fuller, the second and final alert would have been given.

During the following twenty minutes, the outlaws, previously drilled no doubt, would have collected their personal belongings from their rooms. Then they would have been ushered through the trap-door in the lounge to their hiding-place in the tunnel. The rooms they had left would have been quickly tidied by the servants.

Thirty days later, the prisoners were tried at Fort Smith by the judge who had been appointed by Congress to bring much-needed law and order to the 70,000 square miles of Indian Territory. Morgan was called to give evidence. Hanging and custodial sentences were passed, according to the evidence available. Hendrick, among others, was sentenced to death by hanging.

'This is a great day for justice,' declared the judge, when the trial was over. 'At one stroke, eighteen of the most hardened criminals who looked upon the Territory as a safe hiding-place from the law have been removed from society.'

After the trial, Morgan resigned from his job as deputy marshal and rode off to the west.

Marion, her ankle fully healed by now, was tending the small vegetable patch in the garden close to the house, when she saw the distant rider approaching from the east.

She had been watching out for Morgan for some days now, since she had heard from him by telegraph that his mission had been successful. She stood motionless, straining her eyes in the direction of the rider. There was something about the way that he sat erect in the saddle that convinced her that it was Morgan.

She started running towards him, and he quickened the pace of his mount as he saw her approaching. When they met he leapt out of the saddle, took her in his arms, and kissed her.

Ben and Mary Gardner, and their son Joey, working in one of the fields, saw the meeting. The couple smiled at one another.

'I'm glad he's come back to Marion,' said Mary. 'He's a good man.'

Ben Gardner nodded, then called Joey back as the boy started running towards the distant couple.

'It's time,' said Morgan, as he and Marion walked, hand in hand, towards the house, 'that we had that talk about our future.'

'High time,' said Marion.

'Well,' said Morgan, 'I ain't a lawman no more. I've quit the job.'

'I can't say I'm sorry,' said Marion. 'I think I'll be a lot happier married to a man who's around all the time and who ain't liable to get shot in the back any minute.'

'That's what I figured,' said Morgan. 'That's why I've got a proposition to put to you'

'Oh yes,' said Marion. 'What's that?'

'Well,' replied Morgan, 'you know I've got a ranch in Colorado on the Arkansas River, right on the edge of the Rocky Mountains. It's all ready and waiting for us to go along there and run it together as soon as we're married.

'I know you'd miss your folks, but it ain't so far away and the rail tracks are moving westward all the time. Before long, it'll be easy for you to visit the homestead, and maybe Joey could come to Colorado to stay with us for a spell. What d'you think?'

She smiled and kissed him. 'That sounds just fine to me,' she said. 'When do we leave?'

Two weeks later they were married, and on the following day they headed west for the Box C Ranch in Colorado.

The publishers hope that this book has given you enjoyable reading. Large Print Books are especially designed to be as easy to see and hold as possible. If you wish a complete list of our books please ask at your local library or write directly to:

Dales Large Print Books
Magna House, Long Preston,
Skipton, North Yorkshire.
BD23 4ND